NIGHTDIVE

Across the furthest reaches of the Pacific to some of Micronesia's tiniest specks of land, three people are drawn together by circumstances as complex and different as their backgrounds.

Amidst the reefs, the swamps and the remote islands of Palau, an underwater search based on extraordinary information from World War II becomes a search attended increasingly by the intrigue and violence which has shadowed the project almost since its inception one fateful night in Hawaii.

Three people: Daniel Chase, underwater salvage engineer. Lynne Webster, wife of a British marine biologist. John Hyland, adventurer, drifter and onetime aeronautics expert. All of them caught, manipulated and deceived in the recovery of a huge fortune lying somewhere among Palau's strange Rock Islands.

Four million dollars: A stake high enough for men to willingly sacrifice each other in the ruthless fight which Chase and Hyland must win if they are to survive the battle for the consignment waiting on the sea bed.

Nightdive — an account of the greed and treachery of men pitted against each other in one of the world's more lonely places.

NIGHTDIVE

BY

COLIN D. PEEL

ST. MARTIN'S PRESS
NEW YORK

ROBERT HALE & COMPANY
LONDON

© *Colin D. Peel 1977*
First published in the United States of America 1978

All rights reserved. For information, write:
St. Martin's Press, Inc.
175 Fifth Avenue
NEW YORK, N.Y. 10010

Library of Congress Catalog Card Number 77-9120

ISBN 0 312 57278 6

Library of Congress Cataloging in Publication Data

Peel, Colin D
Nightdive.

I. Title.
PZ4.P3738Ni 1978 [PR6066.E36]   823'.9'14   77-9120
ISBN 0-312-57278-6

First published in Great Britain 1977

Robert Hale Limited
Clerkenwell House
Clerkenwell Green
London EC1R 0HT

ISBN 0 7091 6206 5

Printed and bound in Great Britain by
A. Wheaton & Co. Ltd., Exeter

For Anne

ONE

A couple of years ago, I suppose, the distant glimpse of lights would have made something stir inside me. Although I must have flown this route ten or eleven times there's always been that kick at seeing the first glittering pin-pricks of light after crossing nothing but ocean for hours on end.

But this time there was none of the magic, none of the wonder that the Pacific islands have held for me in the past—just a vague emptiness to match the huge expanse of water lying below.

I retrieved my shoes from the mess of hand baggage and crumpled magazines jammed under the seat, put out my cigarette and fastened my seat belt.

Despite the nothing feeling I couldn't resist staring out of the window as the DC 10 banked steeply and the pilot lined us up for the final approach.

Honolulu was a blaze of light now and, for one last moment before we touched down, I searched for the old response to a night landing on Hawaii trying to persuade myself that I could recapture it if I tried hard enough.

With the first bump of the wheels on the tarmac I gave up, knowing what I'd known several months now. Things weren't the same and, if I wasn't careful, there was a chance they might stay that way for a very long time.

Shortly before the aircraft came to rest, the usual scramble began. Grabbing coats, suitcases and cameras, practically all the economy passengers had left their seats unable to wait those last inconsequential minutes before the hatches were opened.

On the other side of the aisle, a denim clad young man had remained seated, his face without expression and an unfinished drink clasped in his hand. Catching my eye he smiled faintly to show he shared my philosophy of waiting until I could disembark without a fight.

When the queue had disappeared I picked up my bag and stood up.

He raised his glass. "If you're thinking of looking for something, there are better places," he said.

I grinned at him. "So you're not getting off."

He shook his head and joined me in the aisle.

"I lied," he said. "This place is like all other places — no better, no worse — just a place."

He smiled again and strode off ahead of me.

Leaving the plane was like walking into a sauna. The sudden transition from cool processed air to the natural Hawaiian variety was not immediately unpleasant but by the time I had crossed the apron and reached the terminal building I was hot and sticky.

Once inside I joined the tail end of the queue for passengers holding non US passports and tried to wake up. Any reasonably long flight seems to dull me whether or not I've managed to snatch a few hours sleep on board and this evening, as usual, I felt pretty lousy when I reached the desk.

"Not your first visit, Mr Chase?" Big and black, the immigration officer was as bored with his job as I was with this tedious part of modern American tradition.

"No," I said, "I'm only stopping over one night this time though."

There was a gleam of interest as he flicked through the passport.

"Been diving in Australia?"

I shook my head. "That's out of date. I haven't been down for a while now."

Our conversation over, he stapled my permit onto one of

the pages and slid the passport back to me across the counter.

A whole hour later, after eventually clearing customs, any trace of residual affection for Honolulu had vanished utterly and the dull feeling had given way to one of irritation.

Passing through the main arrival lounge on the last leg of my journey to the outside world, habitual curiosity made me scan the racks of telegrams clustered on a board just inside the door. And there, clipped half way down the column reserved for people with names beginning with C, was a yellow envelope for Daniel Chase. I was very surprised indeed.

There was no possible reason for anyone to want to get in touch with me that I could think of—in fact, apart from Gerry in London, there wasn't really anyone to contact me whether they had a reason or not.

Beneath my name, the flight number and port of departure made it unmistakably clear that the telegram was intended for me.

I took it from the rack and ripped open the envelope wondering what the hell Gerry had done now. It was from London, but it wasn't from him.

I read it twice:

Please delay departure. Arrive Honolulu Friday Oct. 22nd. Flight 863 from L.A. Gerry Hamill says you will help.

Lynne Webster.

Reading it ten times wouldn't have helped. I had no idea who Lynne Webster might be and I couldn't recall hearing Gerry mention the name, although I knew that didn't mean much. I really didn't want to stay an extra day in Hawaii, either.

Stuffing it in my pocket, I walked out of the building feeling slightly more awake and less annoyed than I had done five minutes ago.

By the time my taxi dropped me outside my hotel in downtown Honolulu I'd read the damn message another three times. As a result I'd just about decided to phone Gerry and ask him what it was all about, but before I'd checked into my room I'd changed my mind.

We — the company that is — couldn't afford international phone calls anymore and, if I knew my brother-in-law as well as I thought I did, there was only the slimmest chance of finding him at the office and an even slimmer chance of finding him at home.

Instead, as soon as I'd dropped my case inside the door, I used the phone to order a beer and a club sandwich from room service then lay full length on the bed to consider Miss or Mrs Webster's request. I must still have been considering when I fell asleep.

A waiter with my order woke me up some minutes later. "Mr Chase?" he asked.

I wished I hadn't arranged to have myself disturbed. "That's me," I said wearily. "Thanks."

"This was at the desk for you." He passed me an envelope.

This time I was surprised enough to forget my manners. He remained hovering in the room whilst I opened the second message I'd received inside the last hour.

Realising my mistake I apologised and gave him a handful of change, waiting for him to leave before taking out the single sheet of paper and unfolding it.

The letterhead informed me that it was from the Japanese embassy in the Philippines and the neatly typed text said that a Mr C. Inahara would be most grateful if I could contact him here in Honolulu after eight in the evening on Friday of this week. A local phone number was given in brackets. The last paragraph was beautiful.

> To be discussed between us is a matter whose value is mutually essential I believe. Reference Mr G. Hamill.

Now it was quite obvious I would have to contact Gerry

even if I had to wait all night to get hold of him. There seemed to be a conspiracy to keep me here another day and even though I was in no particular hurry to go anywhere I wanted some answers.

I asked the operator to place a person to person call to Gerry's home number in Knightsbridge, placed my letter from the unknown Mr Inahara on the bed next to the telegram from the equally unknown Lynne Webster and poured myself a beer.

The whole thing made no sense at all. Firstly, my nice, all expenses paid business trip to Sydney had certainly not been widely publicised if only for the reason that Aqua Engineering was not exactly a well known UK company. Secondly, my hosts the Australian Government had taken pains to keep my visit reasonably quiet for reasons of their own.

Gerry, my only employee or partner, knew roughly where I'd be from time to time during my return to London but, apart from him and a few experts I'd spoken to in Sydney a couple of days ago, no-one should have known or cared that I was here in Honolulu. Both messages seemed to make it clear that my beloved brother-in-law was behind it all, so the sooner I could talk to him the sooner I'd have some idea what all this was about.

I'd eaten my sandwich and finished the beer before the operator called back to say there was no answer from Gerry's number. I asked if she could try in an hour, tried to figure out what time it was in London and fell asleep again.

When I woke up this time, Honolulu sunshine was streaming through the window mixed with noise from traffic in the street below.

I tried to remember whether I'd set my watch to Hawaiian time, couldn't, so reached out for the phone.

"It's nearly eight thirty, sir," the operator replied, "and international called to say your London number has still not been answered."

"What time was that?" I asked her.

"I'm afraid I'm not sure, sir. I've only just come on the desk and all I have are written messages for you."

I might only just have woken up but I didn't miss what she'd said.

"Messages?" I queried. "You've got another one?"

"That's right. A Mr Inahara phoned to say he'd send a car for you at ten o'clock this morning."

I decided I wasn't properly awake after all.

"You're sure he said this morning?" I asked. "Today's Thursday isn't it?"

"It surely is, Mr Chase."

"In that case could you ask room service to send me up enough coffee for about three cups—I think I need them."

"And some breakfast too, sir?"

"Oh, yes please. I'd appreciate some bacon and eggs if that's okay."

"How do you like your eggs, Mr Chase?"

"Anyhow, thanks," I said. "You choose for me, and thanks for the messages."

She said I was welcome and the line went dead leaving me still trying to think.

The letter from the Japanese embassy had suffered a little during the night where I'd slept on it. I smoothed it out on the bedside table, picked the telegram from the floor, then lit a cigarette to help me with my thinking.

Apart from the fact that friend Inahara seemed to have got his dates wrong and had decided not to wait for me to call him, I had no more information to go on than I'd had last night.

I picked up the phone again.

"Yes, Mr Chase?"

"Look," I said, "I'm sorry to be a nuisance but could you ask international to try that London call once more. And while I'm waiting would you get me this local number." I read her the number from Inahara's letter.

"You can call anywhere in Honolulu directly from your room," she said. "But I'll get it for you, if you like—it's no trouble."

"No, that's okay," I said. "I'll just leave you with the London one."

"Thank you, Mr Chase and your eggs will be fried sunny side up."

I grinned, pushed down the button to clear the line and dialled the Honolulu number.

"Kauai Hotel." A girl's voice answered brightly. "Good-morning."

"Goodmorning," I said. "May I speak to Mr Inahara, please."

"One moment, please."

There was a pause, then "Mr Inahara doesn't arrive until tomorrow night, sir. We have a note to collect him from the airterminal at six forty five."

"That's not six forty five this morning?" I asked her.

"No, sir, I have the flight number and arrival time right here."

I thanked her and rang off more confused than ever.

As my breakfast was delivered the phone buzzed. I was beginning to think I might as well keep the damn thing permanently in my hand.

Asking the waiter to leave the tray on the table I grabbed the receiver.

"Is that you, Gerry?" I said.

"No, sir. This is reception again. I'm sorry there's still no reply from England. Should I keep the call in?"

I cursed Gerry silently, wondering who he'd found to spend his time with whilst I was away.

"No, thanks," I said. "I'd better cancel it, I think. I'll try again later."

"How's the breakfast?" She sounded genuinely interested.

I laughed. "It's fine, thanks—but getting cold."

My cigarette had burned to the filter. I stubbed it out and started on the eggs and bacon.

At the end of my second cup of coffee I'd decided.

"It's Daniel Chase again," I said to my friendly operator. "Could you cancel my flight to L.A. for this afternoon, please—and I'd like to extend my reservation here until Saturday." I gave her my flight number.

"How about a new flight booking to L.A., Mr Chase?"

"I'm not sure when I'll be leaving yet but I promise I'll let you make it for me when I go."

"That's nice," she said. "Goodbye."

An hour later, showered and shaved, I put on my last clean shirt, checked my wallet and went downstairs to meet the car. I think I half expected it not to materialise.

Behind the reception desk a pretty girl with thick rimmed glasses smiled pleasantly at me.

"Mr Chase, I presume?" she said.

I returned her smile.

"Have a nice day," she said, moving her eyes towards the door where a thick set Hawaiian in a flowered shirt was standing waiting for someone.

"I'm Chase," I said to him. "Are you from Mr Inahara?"

"Mr Inahara sends his compliments and regrets he was unable to meet you here personally. He is waiting in the office for you."

The speech had been carefully rehearsed to make sure he got it right.

"He is in Honolulu already then?" I said. I received a curt nod in answer to my question.

On the way to the car I tried again. "How far do we have to go?"

"Less than half an hour." He made no effort to meet my eyes.

The car was a brand new Plymouth. I sat in the back and lit another cigarette.

"Mr Inahara apologises for the inconvenience but we

have to collect one other passenger on the way." Another set piece, I thought.

I shrugged. "That's okay, I don't suppose you can tell me what this is all about?"

The lack of reply was not altogether unexpected.

After travelling for three or four miles through heavy traffic the Plymouth drew up outside a small white building with a couple of good sized palms growing out of the lawn in front of it. It was not the Kauai Hotel.

"A moment only." The driver left and made his way over to the main entrance.

He returned a few minutes later accompanied by the casual young man I'd seen on the aircraft last night.

"Small world," I said, offering my hand as he climbed into the car. "My name's Daniel Chase."

He was obviously as astonished to see me as I was to see him, but he recovered quickly enough and the expression of surprise remained on his face for only an instant.

"I'm John Hyland," he said. "You could've saved us both some trouble by speaking to me in Sydney instead of dragging me all the way out here." He smiled. "Unless of course you're really not Inahara in which case I hope you know what the hell is going on because I have not the faintest bloody idea."

As the Plymouth pulled away from the kerb I experienced a vague feeling of disquiet.

"Inahara's asked you to come and see him too?" I asked.

Hyland nodded. "Yeah. He sent me a free ticket for Honolulu and I'm supposed to meet him here tomorrow. Then I get this message that he'll send a car this morning and who should I find in it but you. You're sure you're not Daniel Chase Inahara?"

I shook my head. "My story's pretty much the same as yours, except that I paid my own fare and that I'm on my way back to London."

Hyland wouldn't be older than twenty five and had the easy look about him that I remembered from seeing him on the plane. He was still dressed in faded blue denim.

His speech was that of an American who had either travelled a lot or had spent some time in Australia or the South Pacific. I found it particularly difficult to identify. He appeared to be completely relaxed although I knew he must be as curious about this whole business as I was.

"Do you know where we're supposed to be going?" he asked.

"Inahara's office," I told him. "And that exhausts my information. I don't know what it's all about either. I suppose you don't know someone called Lynne Webster, do you?"

He raised his eyebrows but shook his head. "No."

Our curiosity was partly satisfied when the Plymouth turned onto a tree lined road to the left, entering the courtyard of what looked like an exclusive hotel almost immediately afterwards.

The driver opened the car door for us, indicating that we should follow him.

With answers to our questions only a few minutes away there seemed little point in further speculation. Hyland glanced at me once as we walked towards the swing doors but neither of us spoke.

We were escorted into the building which turned out to be a hotel, as I had first supposed. I made a point of checking that this one wasn't the Kauai, either.

The foyer smelt of the rich exclusivity which you can encounter in pockets all over Honolulu and I thought that the Japanese official we were about to meet must have a pretty substantial expense account. Why he based himself here still remained a mystery.

Our destination proved to be room 12 on the second floor.

"I have been asked to bring you inside," the driver said.

There was something grossly artificial about the way he spoke — as though he'd been taught to say the right thing at the right time. I think Hyland sensed it too. It would be a relief to finally meet this Inahara character and find out why he'd gone to so much trouble to get us both here. Later, much later, I remembered how interested I'd been to meet the man in room 12.

The driver pushed open the door without knocking, holding it politely to allow us to enter the suite ahead of him.

Already I could see enough to know I was just a little out of my class.

For maybe two or three hundred dollars a night anyone could buy this sort of luxury but you have to have a lot of money to want to bother.

Decorated in a tasteful off-white with a wine red coloured carpet thick enough to spend the night on, the hallway we were standing in must have been twenty five feet square. Fluted columns supported an arched roof, also in off-white, and a pair of stone pedestals near the door had what looked like real bronze statuettes sitting on them. The whole atmosphere was one of gracious opulence but someone quite clever had made sure it wasn't overdone.

Even Hyland was impressed. "I'd say Inahara paid for my ticket out of his loose change," he said. "If this is his office I wonder what home is like?"

The driver had closed the door but remained standing behind us as if waiting for something. I wondered if anyone knew we'd arrived.

Then it began.

Unbelievably, from a doorway at the far end of the hall, dressed entirely in black, two men wearing gas masks appeared. Both held what looked like carbon dioxide fire extinguishers.

Mild curiosity of a second before gave way to instantaneous confusion followed by horror.

My yell was drowned by the sound of escaping gas and a thin white cloud gushed out across the room. It wasn't carbon dioxide.

Reflexes learned long ago in the water saved me from the worst of it but I got enough in my lungs to know I had perhaps a minute to live unless I could find some fresh air.

Hyland collapsed at once but the driver was still on his feet, coughing terribly with both hands gripping his throat. His eyes had a funny glaze to them.

There was no time to think.

Holding their tanks at the ready, masked figures were advancing towards me through the gas.

Scared witless and my eyes pouring, I sank to my knees as if on the verge of unconsciousness. I waited until they were close enough then made a spring for one of the statuettes. I felt it cool and heavy in my hand.

My first swing missed the man I'd aimed for but knocked off his gas mask which worked just as well. And then it was hand to hand with the other one, bronze statue against steel gas tank.

Any second now I was going to arrive at the point which most divers have experienced at some time in their life— the time when you can't fight the urge to breathe any longer and give in.

Desperate now, I smashed down hard with the statue, feeling it crunch into the bone of my assailant's shoulder. He squealed like an animal and reeled backwards losing his mask.

I reckoned I had about twelve seconds left.

Grabbing Hyland's jacket with one hand and the door with the other, I pulled both ways at once.

There was a slight escape of gas into the corridor and a draught of fresh air as I stumbled through the door dragging Hyland behind me.

My twelve second estimate had been over generous. I let

everything go and breathed. Then I was sick. All over Hyland.

I slammed the door shut, gulped some more air and fumbled for Hyland's pulse. It was there, but only just.

Five more long deep breaths and I was back inside that beautiful room with the expensive carpet. Gas still hung in the air and there were three bodies on the floor.

Counting in my head, hoping I could hold out, I held the driver's wrist. It was warm by quite lifeless.

I didn't bother checking the other two.

TWO

The apparent lack of serious side affects from whatever gas had been in those tanks was responsible for the fact that we were both sitting here instead of recovering in hospital. Not that Hyland had escaped entirely unscathed.

I watched helplessly as he got up from the bed and went to be sick again.

When he returned he looked slightly better with a trace of colour to his face.

He managed a grim smile. "At least I waited until I got here."

I said nothing, thinking of what had happened since I'd left this room less than an hour ago. The memory was still very fresh.

After discovering the driver dead on the floor I'd stumbled back out into the corridor to find that Hyland had already regained consciousness and was trying hard to sit up. Somehow or other I'd managed to shove his head out of a window at the end of the passageway and hold him long enough for the worst to pass. Later, at his insistence, I'd half carried him and half pushed him downstairs until we reached the foyer where he'd made an enormous effort and walked unsupported out into the street.

A taxi had brought us back here to my hotel and I was now waiting patiently for Hyland to explain his reluctance to call the Honolulu police.

"They'll come looking for us if we don't get hold of them," I repeated. "You know that as well as I do. And I want them to find out why the bloody hell someone has just tried to kill me."

"Us," Hyland coughed. "I thought you looked a selfish bastard."

"If I was that selfish I'd have left you lying on the floor. Come on, give me one good reason why we shouldn't phone them."

He reached into the pocket of his jeans and produced a very crumpled envelope which he handed to me. "I haven't got any sort of reason — just a hunch. Read those."

I withdrew a single sheet of paper and a soiled newspaper clipping. The letter head on the notepaper was familiar. Leaving it for a moment I studied the clipping, reading it carefully to make sure I didn't miss anything.

There wasn't much to miss. It was a brief report about a private aircraft which had disappeared en route from a place called Palau somewhere in the Pacific. An air search had failed to reveal any traces of oil or wreckage and the passengers and crew were feared lost. The last paragraph said a Boeing 727 from Guam was known to have been in the area at about the time the other plane was presumed to have crashed and that the accident could have been caused by trailing vortex turbulence. I wondered what the hell that was.

The letter was less interesting, asking only for John Hyland to fly to Honolulu and suggesting the trip would be valuable to him. Like my letter, the English was atrocious. It was signed by our mutual friend C. Inahara.

"I'm surprised you just got on a plane and came all out here just because someone sent you this," I said. "Didn't you even try and get some more information?"

Hyland lowered himself back onto the bed. "Two years —" he coughed until he was almost completely out of breath. "Two years ago I terminated what I was told was the beginning of a brilliant career in aeronautics in favour of being myself. Just before I chucked it in I wrote a paper on trailing vortex turbulence. Looking back on it I think it was probably quite good. I got offers from all over the place but I'd already decided I'd had enough." He looked me in the eyes. "The funny thing is, though, I didn't lose interest in the subject completely and I guess I might still know more about it than anyone else. There's a chance—a bloody small chance—that if I could get hold of the flight path data for those two planes I could calculate where that one went down."

He was still looking at me and now my own brain was beginning to work.

"We're only alive for one reason," Hyland continued. "Because you used to be a diver. You told me on the way back here in the taxi, remember? That means if I can figure out where the plane hit the water you could find it on the sea bed."

Suddenly everything seemed much clearer. "What do you know about the plane?" I asked. "The one that crashed, I mean."

"Nothing," Hyland said, staring at his hands and then peering closely at my face. "We'd better get these clothes off and have a shower. Look," he pointed at the backs of my hands.

I saw what he meant. My skin had begun to erupt in a rash of thousands of tiny red spots and I could see an artificial flush on Hyland's face now he'd drawn my attention to it.

"You go first," Hyland said, "I'll stay here, just in case."

I hoped the precaution was unnecessary but it seemed sensible to be on our guard. Whoever had squirted nerve gas at us back in that room might decide to try again. The idea made me very uncomfortable.

As I stripped off my clothes, thoughts of the three dead men returned.

"You reckon this'll blow up in our faces if we call the

local police, don't you," I said. "Either that or we'll never find out what it's all about, and you don't want that."

Hyland had his relaxed look back. "When I threw away my career I decided I'd drift for a while. This might just turn out to be what I'm looking for. As long as nobody gets me alone up a dark alley one night I figure it's probably worth staying with it — at least for long enough to see what happens next. That means keeping things quiet."

I said I'd think about what he'd said and went to rinse off my skin in the shower.

The action of high pressure hot water did several things. It removed the smell of fear which had stayed with me since leaving the gas filled room and it allowed me to compare what Hyland had told me with what I myself had deduced from recent events.

There seemed to be no possible doubt that John Hyland and I were about to be recruited to locate a sunken aircraft somewhere in Micronesia. It was also pretty clear that someone wanted us stopped even before we'd been asked to begin.

Areas of skin which had not been completely covered by my clothes were stinging painfully and I started wondering what the gas had done to my insides. Hyland must have been breathing it for some time yet his recovery had been rapid enough, so I supposed the mucous lining to our lungs might have acted as some form of protection.

Why they hadn't tried a more conventional way of getting rid of us I couldn't imagine. Why not simply buy us off? Assuming of course we were going to be offered money for our services.

"Come on," Hyland shouted from the bedroom. "Saving my life doesn't give you any privileges — get out of there."

When I passed him going through the bathroom door he looked much better but his face was an angry red with irritation from the rash.

"Don't call the law until I get out of the shower," he instructed.

I put on some uncontaminated clothes, laid out a spare set for Hyland and decided I'd light a cigarette. It didn't make me cough so things inside couldn't be too bad.

Whilst I waited for my aeronautical friend to have his shower I thought seriously about what he'd told me.

Rather like Hyland, I suppose, up until two years ago I had been close to being an expert in my own field. A field rather different to his. Aqua Engineering had been founded on some very successful deep sea recovery equipment I'd designed myself and things had been all set for the kind of life Jean and I had talked about and planned for so long. Orders had poured in from all over the world for the decompression gear I'd developed and we'd decided our dream had almost come true. Maybe it would've done if Jean hadn't died.

I took a deep draw on the cigarette and switched my mind back to what had happened today. John Hyland had said this could be just what he was looking for—mainly, I guessed, because he was after excitement or adventure for reasons even he probably couldn't explain. Perhaps he was right and perhaps I shouldn't pass up an opportunity to shake myself out of the rut I knew I'd settled into since my wife's death. Sure I'd licked the grief but I hadn't beaten the overwhelming feeling of being cheated and I hadn't managed to climb back to where I'd been when Aqua was half my life and Jean the other.

I was still thinking when Hyland reappeared dripping wet with a smile hovering on his face. He looked much thinner without clothes on but he was well tanned and looked pretty fit for someone who'd been drifting around. He scrubbed himself with the towel.

"Well?" he inquired, "what do you say?"

"I think we both might be messing in something rather nasty."

"But you haven't rejected the idea?"

From the way he said it I knew he was sure he'd got me.

He carried on. "I don't know anything about you — but you pulled me out of that room for which I'm very grateful. The way I see it, I figure that together we should be able to get something worthwhile out of this and even make a little money to cover expenses along the way. That's enough for me — what about you?"

"What's trailing vortex turbulence?" I said.

His smile broadened and he stuck out his hand. "This is the first time I've shaken on a deal stark naked but I'm pleased to meet you, Dan."

"Daniel," I corrected him. "I have a thing about it." I stood up and gripped his hand thinking I was probably being unusually stupid.

I pointed to the clothes. "You'd better put those on, then we'll decide what we're going to do."

When he'd finished dressing I showed him the telegram I'd received from Lynne Webster and my own letter from Inahara.

"And you've never heard of this Lynne Webster?" Hyland asked.

I shook my head. "I tried to phone Gerry — he's my brother-in-law and a partner in Aqua Engineering — but couldn't get hold of him. We'll try again today sometime — he should be able to give us some information, if not the whole story."

"The flight the Webster woman's coming on. What time's it due in?"

I suddenly realised I didn't know. "I'll find out," I said, reaching for the phone.

The girl on the desk wanted to know if my friend was any better. "You can get something sent up for a hangover if you want to," she said. "He looked terrible when you came in."

"Serves him right," I told her. "If he wants to drink all night he must expect to suffer. He's a lot better now, though. I called to ask if you've got an airline time table

there. I have another friend arriving tomorrow—a sober
one. She's on flight 863 from L.A. but I don't know what
time to meet it."

"That's a Pan Am 747, Mr Chase. It's an every day
service from the mainland, I don't need to look it up. Your
friend will be here at around four o'clock tomorrow
afternoon if the plane's on time."

I thanked her and hung up the receiver.

"Four o'clock," I said. "I wonder if she really is mixed up
in all this?"

Hyland looked thoughtful. "If she is, we'll have to hope
she doesn't have an accident before she gets here, won't
we?" he said quietly. "I suppose it depends which side she's
on."

My clothes weren't a bad fit on him in spite of the fact
that he was slightly taller than I. He put on his own shoes
and went to throw his clothes in the bath I'd filled with hot
water.

When he returned I passed him some suntan lotion I'd
bought in Sydney. "Put some of that on your face and
hands—it helps a bit."

"I wonder if anyone's found those bodies yet?" Hyland
said.

I'd been concerned about this ever since we'd arrived back
here. If they had been discovered, there was a chance the
driver could be traced back to one of our hotels where he'd
picked us up. Also, a number of people had seen the dead
Hawaiian with us at the hotel where we'd been attacked.

"I think we'd better go and get a few of your things and
then move on," I said. "I don't mean officially book out of
where we are—I mean vanish—just to be sure."

"And come back to pay our bills when we've made it
rich," Hyland grinned. "Okay, let's do it right away."

Ten minutes later I'd collected sufficient belongings to
half fill my flight travel bag and we were ready to leave. I
left everything else behind in the room.

Downstairs, on the way through the reception lounge I actually felt guilty at walking out without paying. Mostly, I think, because it seemed a shame that the friendly girl behind the desk was going to wind up believing I was a con man. She was going to get an even bigger surprise if the police eventually arrived here looking for me so I supposed there was little point in being concerned. Once having decided to launch out on something I hadn't even dreamed of when I woke up this morning, I knew there was only one way to handle it and that was properly.

I went up to her. "I'm not sure how long I'll be away," I said, "but I'll call for any messages you collect for me as soon as I get in."

Taking off her glasses, she looked at me but obviously decided against saying what she had in mind. Maybe it was something in my eyes. We smiled, then I followed John Hyland out of the door and into what was going to turn out to be a new way of life for me altogether.

We spent the remainder of the day collecting some of John's clothes from his hotel and driving around fairly aimlessly in a rental car looking for a suitable place to spend the night. We talked for much of the time.

By evening we'd learned a lot more about each other and had established an easy friendship — a friendship based on a common attitude to things in general and one which in many ways rather surprised me.

With very little cash between us for embarking on a venture which neither of us understood we decided it would be more economical to sleep in the car. There was the added advantage of instant mobility and we wouldn't have to register at any obscure motel where later someone could remember us.

At six o'clock John parked our Chevrolet outside a small road-house near the Mokapu Peninsula where we stopped talking for long enough to eat our first proper meal of the day.

"I'll phone Gerry again from here," I said. "Unless he's found someone to spend the whole winter with, sooner or later I'm bound to catch him at home."

When I'd finished my coffee I left the table and shut myself in one of the booths near the door. This time, because of my changed financial position, I asked the operator for a collect call.

As usual it took several minutes and a lot of explaining but eventually a girl in London told me the connection had been made.

She came back on the line almost at once to say payment for the call had been accepted. Strangely, the voice that answered was not Gerry's.

Nine thousand miles away someone spoke to me very quietly. I listened to what they had to say then hung up.

My fingers wouldn't work properly and I couldn't get the cigarette out of the packet. When I turned round Hyland was waiting for me to tell him the news.

"Gerry's been murdered," I said.

THREE

Now we were mixing with the crowds in the air terminal, the numbness and feeling of unreality which had followed the news of Gerry's death was gradually fading.

Three hundred passengers arriving on one flight require roughly six hundred people to meet them, and the crush and the noise were what I needed to make me realise that I'd started out on this and what had happened to Gerry made it absolutely certain I was going to have to finish it.

Last night, in the car, I'd told John Hyland a great deal about Jean and about her younger brother. Gerry had been eight years my junior but from the very first time I'd met him we had been more like twin brothers than brothers-in-law. Together we'd shared the early heartaches which had built Aqua into a fairly successful small company and later it had been Gerry who'd gone out and found work for us all over the world. He'd had a natural ability to get on with people which, time and time again, had paid off when we'd been competing for a diving job against companies with more experience and better equipment.

Gerry Hamill had been a fine young man, my brother-in-law and my friend. Someone had killed him and, when I found out who it was, they were going to pay for what they'd done. I couldn't bring Gerry back to life but I swore I'd avenge his death.

For a good part of the night John Hyland had listened to me with commendable patience whilst I'd alternated between sorrow and anger trying to come to grips with the tragic fact that Gerry had been murdered.

Curiously, the bitterness which finally settled on me had seemed to meet with Hyland's approval, probably, I realised now, because it reinforced my earlier resolve to join him in the venture to uncover the truth behind the events which had led to our association.

There was no doubt in either of our minds that Gerry had become a victim of the same plot which had nearly cost us our own lives here in Honolulu. John had come up with a couple of unlikely theories of what could be behind it all, but I think we both knew we were going to need a lot more information before we could even begin to make intelligent guesses. He'd kept me talking and smoking until well past midnight but I hadn't fallen asleep until the early hours of the morning. In retrospect he'd obviously done his best to ease the grief and I'd been grateful for his company. I still was.

Right now he was busy trying to identify Lynne Webster among the crowd filing through the door of the arrival lounge.

He pointed to a blonde with most of her chest propped up on a suitcase as she wheeled an overloaded luggage trundler towards the nearest telephone kiosk.

"What do you think?" he asked.

"Lynne Webster will be brunette, cool and carry one small expensive suitcase," I told him. "You read the wrong kind of books."

Ten minutes and a hundred passengers later John nudged my arm to draw attention to a woman fitting my description remarkably well. She was standing alone to one side of the main stream of people and was stooping down to check a strap on her case. It looked like a small expensive case.

"If you meant what you said you'd better go over and say hello," he said grinning. "My money's on that sleek number over there." He inclined his head in the direction of a good looking woman who was obviously looking for someone who was here to meet her.

"Okay," I said. "You'd better use my name when you introduce yourself, though, otherwise you'll get nowhere even if you're right."

He nodded and began threading his way across the hall. When he reached her I saw him say something. For his trouble he received a quick smile accompanied by a shake of her head.

Returning my attention to the woman matching the description I'd invented, I noticed she'd finished what she was doing and was walking towards the main exit.

Hurriedly I moved to intercept her, wondering if I'd guessed correctly.

"Excuse me," I said, "you're not Lynne Webster are you?"

Dark brown eyes inspected me impersonally.

"Mr Chase?" she asked. "Mr Daniel Chase?"

I decided I must be cleverer than I thought. I smiled and shook her hand. It was quite cool and, as far as I could tell, the hand of a woman perfectly confident at meeting a complete stranger. Later I would realise the confidence was largely artificial.

"Oh, I'm so pleased you're here," she said. "I wasn't sure whether you'd get my cable or if you'd decide to wait until I arrived. When I didn't hear any announcement on the PA system and there wasn't a note or anything I thought you must have already left for London. I really am very grateful you waited. How on earth did you know who I was?"

Lynne Webster had a fine boned face, a pretty mouth and very long dark brown hair to match her unusual eyes. I guessed her to be about thirty with plenty of money. She wore a wedding ring and had a look about her that I've always associated with those well bred women which England produces so easily.

"You match your name," I said. "But I guessed too. I'm sorry I didn't think of having you called, though. I got your cable of course — that's why I'm here."

John Hyland interrupted us. He had a huge grin on his face. "I sure must start reading your kind of books," he said.

I introduced him.

"I thought you were here alone, Mr Chase," she said. "Mr Hamill said you were on your way back from business in Sydney."

"John's a friend of mine," I said. "And I think I'd better tell you right away—I'm afraid Gerry Hamill's dead. I heard last night."

The shock showed all over her. I watched whilst she struggled to overcome it, admiring the speed at which she recovered.

"I'm terribly sorry," she said. "Please can we leave here and find somewhere quieter to talk? I must explain why I sent you the cable."

John took the case from her. "We could use some answers," he said easily. "I hope you've got some for us, Mrs Webster."

She chose not to answer him and accompanied us without speaking to the parking area where we'd left the Chevrolet.

John walked on ahead a short way to check over the car. Both of us had admitted to being a trifle nervous and last night we'd decided there was no harm in being careful. Now Lynne Webster was here things might either become more dangerous or much safer—everything depended on what she had to tell us and whether she was involved with Inahara.

"What is Mr Hyland doing?" she inquired.

"I'll explain later," I said. "I'm afraid we're going to have to talk in the car—at least to start with, anyway. We'll go somewhere and park if that's okay?"

She nodded her agreement but I thought I detected a trace of apprehension on her face as she slid into the front seat. There was no real hesitation though so I could easily have imagined it.

"Where to, Daniel?" John asked.

"Anywhere reasonably quiet where we can pull off the road."

Lynne Webster was obviously tired and I sensed she was uneasy at being driven to some possibly deserted roadside parking area.

"Are you sure we couldn't go to your hotel?" she asked. "I'd very much prefer to clean up and stop moving for a while."

"Look, I really am sorry," I said, "but we have a problem. I'd rather not say anything about it until I know what you want to see me about. I realise that doesn't make any sense, but it might later on. Please believe it's better to stay out of town until we've had a talk."

Hyland forestalled her next remark. "Maybe you should explain that you and I are working together," he said without turning in his seat.

"That's right, you can say anything you like to both of us. I have no idea what you want but, whatever it is, you can rely on us to keep our conversation absolutely confidential."

John swung the car out onto the road to Diamond Head with one eye on the mirror. Just for a second I thought he might have done this sort of thing before but quickly put the notion to the back of my mind. He was only taking the precautions we'd discussed earlier and so far we'd learned nothing to indicate we were being unnecessarily wary. With any luck we'd discover very shortly if the danger was imagined of not.

Whilst we travelled I considered my first impression of Lynne Webster deciding eventually that it was too early to form an accurate opinion. Only one thing made me wonder about her. Understandably, Mrs Webster had been surprised to be asked to do her explaining in a car but her severe reaction to the news of Gerry's death and her subsequent behaviour seemed to indicate she was less surprised than I would have expected.

A short way into the Kapiolani park, before we reached Diamond Head, John found an unoccupied layby far enough off the road for us to talk comfortably without the interruption of traffic noise.

The afternoon was pleasantly warm and the three of us left the car to lean on some railings lining the cliff top. The view out over the Pacific was tremendous.

"Okay," I said. "I was scheduled to fly out of here yesterday. You sent me a cable saying my brother-in-law believed I'd help you. So I've delayed leaving to hear what it is you want me to help you with."

I offered her a cigarette but she shook her head and stared out to sea for a moment.

"Don't forget we've got to phone Inahara later on," John reminded me.

Although I was watching her closely, I detected no sign that she recognised the name.

Still half facing the ocean she began speaking.

"Mr Chase," she said hesitantly. "I really don't know how to explain why I'm here. It's so awfully complicated and now I find you did wait for me after all I feel a little embarrassed at having sent the cable. You see, I haven't done anything like this before."

I lit my cigarette and waited.

"Tell us why you went to see Gerry Hamill in London," Hyland prompted.

She nodded. "A friend of mine who knew Gerry said he might be able to help me because he knew the Pacific islands well. I went to see him and he suggested I tried to meet you in Honolulu. You see I'm really on my way to Palau."

I saw a faint flicker in Hyland's eye.

"What for?" I said.

"That's a hard question to answer," she grimaced briefly. "I'll have to go back about eight months— February, I think it was. Noel, my husband, came home one night and said he'd been offered an opportunity to carry out some new research work in the Pacific—he's a marine biologist. We argued about it for days. Noel had always wanted to go on a trip like the one he described to me but we'd previously decided to start a family about the same time as he received the offer and I wasn't prepared to put it off any longer." She smiled slightly. "I'm not as young as I was and, to be blunt, I was tired of taking second place to my husband's career."

She turned her back on the sea as if to indicate she had closed that particular chapter on her life.

"I won't bore you with that," she said. "Noel left England two months ago and arrived in Palau in mid August to join a research team already working there. At least that's what he told me."

"What does that mean?" I asked.

"I don't really know myself," she said. "He sent me a short letter—the first of several. It was from Guam saying he hoped to start work out on the Rock Islands in about a week. The Rock Islands lie just south of Koror in the Palau district—that's about all I know about them apart from being able to point to them on a map.

Later he sent me two more letters, both from Palau; I've brought them with me if you want to read them. The last one arrived at the end of September." She smiled the same smile. "In case you're going to ask, the answer is my husband tends to become very involved with his work. One or two letters a month would be par for the course as far as Noel's concerned.

I hadn't expected him to be away from England for such a long time but he said the weather had been bad and the project was behind so I didn't worry too much. His last letter sounded a bit strange. There were pages and pages of it telling me about what he had planned for us when he got home—not like Noel at all. I thought nothing of it then except that it was peculiar for him to ramble on so much."

Hyland interrupted. "But something happened to make you change your mind?"

She nodded. "A number of things. Firstly a letter arrived addressed to Noel from Switzerland. I opened it and found out it was from a bank in Geneva. They wanted to know the number of his account in Palau. Then, a few days later, a statement from the same bank was delivered — by hand, I think. It wasn't postmarked and it didn't have a stamp on it. It showed a credit in my husband's name for ten thousand American dollars."

She turned to face me. "Marine biologists don't earn that sort of money suddenly, Mr Chase — not even the very best ones."

"And even if they do, they don't put it into a Swiss bank," I remarked.

"I come from a very wealthy family, Mr Chase. Noel has always tried to live up to a standard he believed I wanted." The half smile returned for an instant. "If I'd wanted to marry a rich husband I wouldn't have chosen a marine biologist, but I have never ever been able to convince him that money is of no interest to me. I wondered if he'd become involved in something illegal to try to show me — —" her voice tailed off.

"What did you do?" John asked.

"I wrote to Noel at once asking what the money was for but I didn't get an answer so I sent a cable to the hotel he was supposed to be staying at in Koror. A week later when I'd received no reply I started to get really worried and began trying to find out more about the research trip. I think that's when everything seemed to start going completely wrong.

I discovered Noel had resigned from his position at the laboratory where he worked and no-one there knew anything about his trip to Palau. He'd lied about everything to me, and someone had paid ten thousand dollars into a secret account in Geneva."

Hyland was trying not to look too pleased as she unfolded her story. Even I was conscious of growing curiousity or excitement at what she was telling us. I stubbed out my cigarette and waited for the rest of it.

She continued immediately. "I eventually found out Noel had never been heard of at the hotel on Koror and I began to wonder if he'd really gone to Palau at all. Then, about ten days ago, I had a visit from a Japanese gentleman at home. He said he'd come to see Noel. When I told him he was still on Palau—even though I wasn't sure anymore—he shook his head and said something about a plane which I couldn't understand properly. I almost begged him to tell me what he wanted and where I could find my husband but he refused. By then I was close to desperation and I can't tell you the relief I felt when I received another letter from Noel the next morning."

She opened her handbag as if to take it out but changed her mind at the last minute.

"Just tell us about it," I prompted.

"The postmark's all smudged and I can't read the date," she said, "but I think it's from a place called Babelthuap. I looked it up on a map and it's the main island in the Palau group. The letter's very short. It says they've found the submarine but the danger he told me about is growing all the time."

I exchanged glances with John.

"And he never mentioned submarines or danger in the other letters he sent?" I asked.

"No, but I'm sure now he sent me one which never arrived. I think he must have written to me and explained what he's actually been doing there—he may even have sent several letters." She spread her hands in a gesture of hopelessness. "I didn't get them."

By now I'd understood why Gerry had suggested she try and contact me in Hawaii. He would've been pretty sure a story like Lynne Webster's would have interested me and that I might have been willing to offer some sort of assistance whilst I was still in the Pacific region. Perhaps Gerry had thought there was a job for Aqua in the offing.

"Is there anything else?" I said. "Apart from your decision to fly out to Palau to try to find your husband, I mean."

She nodded. "A letter from the Japanese embassy in London. Well, not a letter really—a press cutting about a light plane that had crashed somewhere near Palau. I went to ask them why they'd sent it but I couldn't find anyone there who'd speak to me about it. That's when I went to see your brother-in-law."

"Do you believe your husband was on the plane?" Hyland asked quietly.

Her composure gone, she spun round to face him. "I don't know. I don't know anything. Can you imagine how it feels, Mr Hyland? I don't think you can—nobody can." She looked out to sea again.

I wanted to say something reassuring but couldn't find the words.

"You told Gerry Hamill all of this?" I asked.

"Yes." She remained standing with her back to me. "He said he'd see what he could discover for me by telephoning around."

"Did anyone else know about the last letter—the one mentioning the submarine?" I said. "And who knew you were coming out here to look for him?"

"No-one and no-one, Mr Chase. I decided it would be better to keep the whole thing to myself. Will you please answer some of my questions now?"

"Yes, I will."

Slowly she turned to face me. Her face was pale and her lips were firmly compressed. "What happened to Mr Hamill?"

"He was murdered. I talked to the London police last night. I don't know how but I think I could take a guess at why—now I've heard what you have to say."

She made no comment but asked her next question. "Will you help me?"

"Yes."

"And you Mr Hyland?"

John nodded at her. "Three heads are a hell of a lot better than one. I'd decided half way through your story — so had Daniel. Daniel and I have our own reasons for wanting to help, anyway, but we can tell you about those later. Right now we'd better drive back into town. Believe it or not, Daniel and I have both been asked to telephone someone from the Japanese embassy in the Philippines who arrives here in Honolulu this evening."

"Someone called Inahara?" she asked.

"Yes," I said. "Do you know the name?"

"No, Mr Chase. I heard Mr Hyland mention it before, that's all. Is this person connected with what I've told you?"

"Almost certainly. You see John was sent the same newspaper cutting and both of us have been asked to contact Inahara here in Honolulu."

Her brown eyes widened. "So you were involved before I sent my cable?"

"No, Mrs Webster. It's all happened at once. If I'd carried straight on to London as I originally planned I'd probably never have become involved at all."

She reached out and placed a hand on my arm. The self assurance was barely discernable now.

"Mr Chase, I didn't say thank you for your offer of help — or to you Mr Hyland. I am so very — so very grateful. I can't tell you how much it means. I only hope everything will be alright."

So do I, I thought, so do I.

FOUR

It was nine o'clock when we arrived back in town. The evening was warm and the soft glow of lights filtering through the palms and shrubs surrounding nearly every house and hotel would have made Honolulu a pleasant place to be if circumstances had been different. Another time perhaps I'd have gone for a stroll, enjoyed a quiet drink and found somewhere out of the way to have dinner. But tonight I had an appointment.

Although John and I were hungry, having eaten nothing but a few sandwiches all day, we'd decided to make our respective phone calls to Inahara before doing anything else in order to give ourselves maximum thinking time.

We chose a roadside phone box on Ala Wai Boulevard as a suitable place from which to make the first one. Hyland parked the Chevrolet a short way down the road from it and switched off the engine.

"If things sound okay, I'll mention that you and I are already acquainted," I said. "But unless I'm absolutely sure, it'd be better for you to phone him separately in a couple of hours time so he doesn't suspect anything."

"I don't honestly believe those guys in the gas-masks had anything to do with Inahara," Hyland said. "He wasn't scheduled to arrive in Honolulu until this evening according to the hotel you phoned and I can't see why the hell he'd have bothered to get me all the way here just to kill me."

"But the taxi driver used his name," I reminded him. "There's a connection somewhere so let's wait and see before we make up our minds."

42

Lynne Webster spoke to me as I got out of the car. "Are you going to tell him I'm here with you if you decide he's on our side?"

"I don't know. We wouldn't gain anything by it so it might be more sensible to meet him before we tell him what's happened."

Once inside the call box I laid Inahara's letter on the shelf beside the receiver whilst I inserted the coins and dialled the number of the Kauai Hotel.

The receptionist answered.

"May I speak to Mr Inahara, please?" I asked.

There was a muffled burring followed by a click as the room extension was picked up.

"Inahara?" I inquired.

"It is. To whom am I speaking, please?" The English was excellent with a merest trace of an oriental accent. It didn't seem to match the rather poor quality of the grammar in the letters John and I had received.

"This is Daniel Chase. You asked me to phone you."

"Ah, Mr Chase. I am delighted you have stayed in Honolulu. You received my letter of course?"

"Yes, I did. Can we discuss it over the telephone or would you prefer to meet me somewhere?"

There was a slight pause before he answered. "Mr Chase, there is another gentleman who I have also asked to meet me here—a Mr John Hyland. I do not yet know if he has accepted my invitation to come to Hawaii. I would prefer to wait perhaps one hour to see if he will call me. If he does then the three of us could have dinner together, if it is not too late. But you have eaten already, I expect?"

"No," I replied. "And by coincidence I've already met Mr Hyland—we travelled here on the same plane from Sydney."

There was no hesitation from Inahara. "That is splendid, Mr Chase, if you know where he is staying would you be kind enough to ask him to get in touch with me immediately. No, no—I must not put you to the bother. I will contact him myself if you will tell me the name of his hotel."

I made up my mind. "He's here with me now. If it's okay with you we could both meet you for dinner in say half an hours time."

"There is somewhere you can recommend where we can talk, Mr Chase? My local knowledge is, I am sure, inferior to your own."

I gave him the name of a small restaurant John and I had selected earlier in the day to guard against an invitation to Inahara's hotel.

"It's on Kalakau Avenue," I said. "I imagine a taxi would be the easiest way for you to get there."

"Shall we say nine thirty, Mr Chase? That is convenient for you?"

"That'll be fine," I said. "I look forward to meeting you."

I hung up and returned to the car where I relayed the news to John and Lynne.

"You're sure?" Hyland queried when I told him of the arrangements.

"No, of course I'm not bloody sure. But he sounded on the level so I made the decision. Nothing much can go wrong in the middle of Honolulu at this time of the evening, anyway."

Mrs Webster seemed more at ease now we'd established contact with the mysterious Inahara. "And am I included in your dinner invitation? Or do I have to sit outside in the car?"

John grinned at her. "We'll smuggle a steak out for you."

"I can't see any reason why we shouldn't all go," I said. "I think we might just as well come out in the open right away."

She sighed. "I feel very unliberated the way you're speaking about me. I'm not certain if I'm being protected or ignored." She smiled at me. "Perhaps there's something I should make clear."

During the drive back from Kapiolani park, John and I had told her of our letters from Inahara and about yesterday morning's attempt on our lives. She'd listened to all we had to say without interruption until we'd described the surprise gas attack in the hotel. It had shocked her considerably and I think it was that, coupled with Gerry's death, that finally convinced her we'd all become caught up in much more than a search for her missing husband. It was now obvious that Noel Webster had been working on something very dangerous indeed and the realisation of how dangerous had raised all sorts of doubts in her mind. I knew she'd have to re-think the whole situation in view of what she'd learned and I anticipated a flood of questions before she would decide what to do.

"There are probably a lot of things we haven't mentioned," I said. "But we'll get around to them. Is there anything important you haven't told us though?"

"Mr Chase, you and Mr Hyland— —." I stopped her by raising my hand in protest.

"Look," I said. "I know we don't know each other very well and I know you and I are English, but all this Mr and Mrs business is stupid: I'm Daniel, John is John and we'd like to call you Lynne as long as you don't mind."

"I suppose it would be easier," she agreed. "What I wanted to say simply concerned money. If you're both going to help me find Noel I'm sure we'll have to spend several days on Palau and we have to get there first. I want you to understand I'm prepared to cover all of the costs. I hope you don't mind me bringing it up. I just wanted you to know." She finished speaking rather lamely.

"Hired hands?" John said without thinking.

"No, John. Friends. I mean that."

She swivelled round in her seat to face me. "I don't believe you're the sort of men who'd be prepared to work as hired hands. You said you'd help me, didn't you?" She sounded strained. "I wish I hadn't said anything. Oh,

please don't laugh at me." She covered her face and turned
away.

Hyland knew it was his fault but he was smart enough to
keep quiet until she dropped her hands and fumbled in her
handbag for a handkerchief. I wished I hadn't grinned at
her.

"God, I wish this had never begun," she said. "Why
couldn't things have gone on without this happening —
why?"

I lit a cigarette and thought about the life of a wealthy
woman married to a marine biologist, wondering what her
husband was like and whether their marriage had been any
good. The fact that she'd decided to try and locate him on
Palau was some sort of answer but I wasn't sure yet what
kind of woman she really was. And I had a nasty suspicion
we were going to find Noel Webster in a smashed up
aircraft on the bottom of the Pacific underneath a lot of
water.

Once or twice, she herself had referred to her husband
in the past tense, correcting herself quickly as if trying to
put such thoughts to the back of her mind, so I knew she
must have her own doubts about whether he was still alive.

"Lynne," Hyland said gently, using her christian name
for the first time. "You know we weren't laughing at you.
You're all worked up because you've found out this isn't just
a straightforward search for your husband. I think you
might have known that for a while, anyway. We don't know
what's going to happen but it's a hell of a lot better for the
three of us to work on it together. And sure we're friends.
With old Daniel here we'll sort it out — I promise you."

"Old Daniel?" I queried. "Who was it who pulled you
out of the gas?"

"Old Daniel — who else?"

I leaned forward in my seat. "The first time I saw you,
you told me that if I was looking for something there were
better places — remember?"

He shrugged. "So I was right, or wrong, depending how you look at it. Mostly I'm wrong, though. Come on, let's get on over to the restaurant and have a drink." He started the car, did a rapid U turn and headed in the direction of Kalakau Avenue.

Cars were parked bumper to bumper all along the street when we arrived and it was clear that we'd chosen a popular watering hole for both local residents and tourists.

The Koko restaurant was a small eating establishment situated on the corner of a narrow side road running alongside the Ala Wai canal. We drove around the neighbourhood for a while eventually beating another car into a vacant parking slot by a matter of seconds.

The short walk to the Koko increased our thirst and I began to hope we'd arrive before Inahara so I could down a couple of whiskies and so Lynne could unwind.

We pushed through a hanging bamboo curtain to enter the restaurant and headed directly for the bar.

At once a large man left his table and walked over to us carrying his drink.

"Please excuse me," he said, "is one of you gentlemen Mr Daniel Chase?"

I recognised his voice from my recent telephone conversation. "I am," I said. "You must be Mr Inahara."

There was the suggestion of a bow. "I too arrived early." He shook hands with me and turned to Lynne.

"May I introduce Mrs Webster," I said. "She's a friend of mine from England."

Another bow accompanied by a faint expression of disapproval or annoyance as he shook her hand.

"And John Hyland from Australia, of course. I am delighted to meet all of you. Please allow me to order your drinks."

I'd come across a number of Japanese over the years and I have visited Japan twice. Because of that I knew the popular European conception of the stature of the Japanese people was largely incorrect. Nevertheless, even compared with some of the more solid characters I'd met, Inahara was large. He was no taller than John but extremely wide without an ounce of fat on him. I studied him more closely whilst he ordered a Campari soda for Lynne and whiskies for John and me.

About forty with an uncharacteristically craggy face, I thought he would have made one hell of a Samuri warrior in the good old days before Japan had decided it was time to be discovered by the west.

He passed me my drink, the glass almost entirely obscured by his hand.

"I am not what you expected?" he inquired.

I grinned. "A lot of Europeans must have said that to make you ask."

"One learns not to expect anything. Nowadays it is not to which race you belong that matters but what values you have decided to adopt. The choice is very wide."

The remark seemed deliberately provocative so I ignored it. "My Japanese is lousy," I said. "In fact that's a lie—it's non existant. Your English is perfect—your speech, I mean. So why, if you don't mind me asking, was your letter so — —."

"Quaint is perhaps the word? Have I chosen correctly? Because, Mr Chase, someone else in the embassy wrote your letter—and the one to Mr Hyland, both, however, on my behalf. I have been very busy and requested my embassy to deliver your letters for me. I will explain later. Now, before we talk, may I ask if you travelled here by taxi?"

"No," John answered, "we're using a hire car. Why?"

"I see. And it is parked nearby?"

"Fairly," I said. "Why do you want to know?"

"A precaution, Mr Chase, no more than that. You will excuse me for one moment, please."

He left the bar and approached a table near the

entrance where a young man and a girl were talking. After
speaking to them the girl walked back with him to the bar.
Inahara didn't introduce her.

"Mr Hyland, would you please explain where you have
left your car and describe its colour and make."

Very puzzled, John gave her the information, reading off
the registration number from the key ring provided by the
hire company.

The girl thanked him, returned to her boyfriend and the
pair of them left the restaurant immediately.

"Now," Inahara smiled. "Another drink or would you
prefer to eat?"

"I think we'd prefer answers more than anything," I
said. "But if Lynne doesn't mind, maybe we could talk
over dinner."

"That would be nice," Lynne said. "Please tell us why
you wanted John to tell that girl about our car."

"You will understand more easily when you have heard
what I have to say to you," Inahara replied. "I must
confess I am surprised to find you in Honolulu, Mrs
Webster."

He led us to a table in an alcove at the rear of the room,
holding Lynne's chair for her and beckoning to the waiter
who was hovering ready with the menus.

We ordered right away, all of us anxious for Inahara to
begin his explanation.

"I will start by demonstrating that I have undertaken my
background work thoroughly," he said. "If I have obtained
information which is incorrect, please interrupt me."

He used a match from one of the complimentary books
lying in the ash tray to light my cigarette for me.

"Mr Chase. Owner of Aqua Engineering in London, a
small company specialising in underwater work and a
holder of three world patents on diving equipment which
allows me to work at depths up to one thousand feet. Your
experience in the Pacific is not inconsiderable although

you have worked in many of the world's oceans. Your wife is dead and you and your late brother-in-law have run the company alone for the past few years."

I wasn't really surprised he'd heard about Gerry. As he'd said, he'd done his homework well. I didn't bother to ask him how he knew Gerry was dead.

He turned to John. "And Mr John Hyland. An acknowledged authority on trailing vortex turbulence, one of the phenomena associated with the aerodynamics of jet aircraft. I understand it has something to do with the lift generated by the wing profile which creates dangerous air turbulence extending for as far as ten miles behind a modern plane. You, Mr Hyland, a gifted young man, have elected to join the ranks of those who prefer not to work on research but to dissipate their energies." He lifted a hand. "I am not moralising, I am stating fact.

Mr Chase has been in Sydney advising the Australian Government on techniques for vacuum or suction mining of manganese nodules lying on the sea bed off the west coast.

You, Mr Hyland, to my good fortune, have just completed a two week visit to New Zealand where you have been advising a company on modifying the design of a new hang glider of remarkable performance. I was able to locate you in Sydney on your return through one of my Australian colleagues.

I also know, of course, that both of you gentlemen have joined forces. I should perhaps have been more honest to you on the telephone, Mr Chase, but I did not want to alarm you."

He smiled charmingly at Lynne. "Finally we come to Mrs Webster, the wife of Noel Webster currently believed to be in the West Caroline Islands on Palau. I regret my interest has been principally directed towards the activities of your husband and I was not expecting to meet you here. However, I am sure you have associated yourself with Mr Chase in an endeavour to locate your missing husband."

I raised my glass. "Wonderful," I said with as much cynacism as I could muster. "You must have spent a hell of a lot of time and money finding out all that."

"I trust you are not genuinely offended, Mr Chase. The Japanese Government is prepared to spend a great deal of money on the project which concerns me."

John Hyland appeared unimpressed with Inahara's condensed history. He waited for our entree to be delivered before making one of his typically blunt remarks.

"How much did it cost your Government to kill Gerry Hamill?" he asked.

Inahara answered him calmly. "I think you must know your question is directed at the wrong person. Similarly, the unfortunate attempt on the lives of yourself and Mr Chase here in Honolulu was of course organised by what I can only term my opposition. I only regret I did not forsee the danger. We must hope it will not happen again."

He stopped talking in order to attend to his plate of oysters leaving John, Lynne and me to our own thoughts until he had finished. I realised we hadn't learned anything new yet.

Two waiters arrived shortly after we'd finished our first course. One to remove the empty plates, the other to serve the lobsters we'd ordered as a main meal.

Inahara embarked on the next part of his story as his huge hands began tearing one of the lobsters to pieces.

"Over thirty years ago, on the tenth of August, nineteen forty five, four days after the first atomic bomb was dropped on Hiroshima and the day after the second bomb was dropped on Nagasaki, a number of influential men in Japan—the Emperor among them—gathered for a high level meeting in Tokyo. After several hours discussion they concluded that Japan would inevitably have to surrender to the Americans or suffer total obliteration by the new weapon which had been used so cruelly on my countrymen. I expect you have read of the meeting I have described.

At that time, with over a hundred thousand people dead, it was not unreasonable for the men at that meeting to also conclude that the Japan they knew would disappear forever during the subsequent occupation by the allied powers.

In short, gentlemen and Mrs Webster, being Japanese who had lived more by the old ways than by what we regard as the new, they believed that Japan was utterly ruined. In an attempt to preserve something of their heritage before the occupation, they decided to arrange to gather a number of priceless works of art from various places in the country and ship them overseas to a safe resting place."

Already, everything was falling neatly into order for me. Inahara must have sensed I'd guessed the truth about the submarine before I had time to speak.

He lifted a choice piece of lobster on his fork and smiled at me with all of his beaten up face.

"Not quite, Mr Chase. I think you are being a trifle too hasty. It is my fault for being imprecise. You are correct if you have guessed that a submarine was scheduled for the job — it left Japan bound for Europe on August the twenty fifth in nineteen forty five carrying a shipment of such value that it is doubtful if we could comprehend how many dollars it would take to buy it today.

There is, however, something I have neglected to mention. Between August the tenth and August the twenty fifth — the time when the cargo was being made ready — four other men who were not present at the meeting in Tokyo accidentally learned of the secret arrangements.

Being perhaps less typical than other members of my race, these men used their influence to include very substantial portions of their own personal fortunes in the official containers carrying the works of art. For obvious reasons they made certain their currency would be internationally negotiable and this was done very simply, gentlemen. In each container, four in all, a sealed compartment was constructed large enough to hold about a million dollars worth of diamonds by today's values. You will note I have said four containers."

John had stopped eating several minutes ago. "Four million bucks worth of diamonds," he said quietly. "You're kidding."

"I most certainly am not, Mr Hyland. A year ago, information became available following the death of the last of the four men who had secreted such wealth on board the submarine. It is irrefutable."

All of us started to speak at once. Lynne won the contest.

"Why on earth didn't they try and get their diamonds back from the sunken submarine after the war?" she asked.

"I see that you have already surmised the submarine never reached its destination. The answer to your question is very simple, Mrs Webster. The route of the submarine had been known only to a handful of officials, the Emperor and the crew who of course died when the vessel sank. By the time relations with the Americans had reached a point where the cargo of art works could have been retrieved even if the submarine could have been located, they would have been ruined either by the action of sea water should the hull have been holed, or by condensation if it had not. Officially, there was no point whatever in searching for the sunken vessel.

For the men whose diamonds were on board, the situation was very awkward. In order to discover the most likely resting place of the submarine they would have had to ask embarrassing questions in official circles which could easily have revealed their motives. In Japanese society, the

dicovery of such motives would be regarded as the equivalent of treason. Thus, they were trapped by their own
greed."

Lynne nodded. "So no-one else knew about the diamonds
until last year?"

"That is correct. An interesting story is it not?"

I busied myself with my lobster mulling over what
Inahara had just told us. Even John was silent as he
reviewed the incredible background to the letters Inahara
had sent.

So now I knew what it was all about. Well nearly. I was
on the point of breaking the silence and asking my next
question when the girl who'd been given details about our
car approached the table.

She said something to Inahara in what sounded like
fluent Japanese. He looked grave then extracted a hundred
dollar note from his wallet and gave it to her. In return he
received a length of thread, a strong rubber band and a
pencil.

She asked him a question which made him point to me
and shake his head. The girl smiled briefly at us then
walked away.

"Who the hell is she?" John asked.

"In English I think she would be called a guardian
angel," Inahara said. "Is that correct?"

"I don't know," I said. "I thought guardian angels
worked for free."

"Ah, Mr Chase, I fear those days are gone forever, but a
hundred dollars is cheap enough, I think."

"For what?" Lynne said, pointing at the pencil on the
table. "For those things?"

"No, Mrs Webster, for your life."

FIVE

I could almost imagine that everyone else in the restaurant had stopped talking too. There was an astonished expression on Lynne's face and Inahara's last remark had even surprised the normally imperturbable John Hyland.

"Cut it out, Inahara," John said. "Come on, what did the girl say?"

Our Japanese host pushed his plate of broken lobster shell away and wiped his mouth carefully with a table napkin.

"I believe recent occurrences may have made you suspect that a search for the missing diamonds is being carried out by two opposing organisations. One of these, of course, is the Japanese Government who consider that four million dollars should not be left lying on the sea bed when it could be usefully but discreetly employed inside the Japanese economy. The other organisation is of British origin and has been working secretly for several months in order to locate the submarine before anyone else. They are a private group of men, utterly unprincipled and prepared to go to any extreme.

As an indication of how determined they are, I have to tell you they have just wired a package of explosives to the ignition circuit of your car."

There was another stunned silence around the table.

"The girl," I said. "You asked her to watch the car?"

"Indeed, Mr Chase. I was followed here, as I thought, and our friends with the explosives must have been waiting for you to join me. To make quite certain you and Mr

Hyland cannot lend your skills to my project, they have decided to try and eliminate you for the second time."

"Christ!" John said. "These guys really don't mess around, do they. Did you expect this sort of thing to happen?"

Inahara nodded. "I approached Mr Hamill in London to explain the position of my Government. Mr Hamill is now dead. I also approached both you gentlemen and have been informed by my contacts here in Honolulu that you narrowly escaped a similar fate on Thursday morning. You will tell me about it later, I trust. Now the same people have cleverly arranged to incinerate you in your car—they are obviously very anxious to delay me."

"I'm not so much worried about your delay," I said with genuine feeling. "It's the idea of being blown to bits I don't like."

"Ah yes, Mr Chase. I put it badly—please forgive me."

We'd all forgotten Lynne. She'd gone pale and was sitting very upright in her seat.

"It's okay, Lynne," I said. "Now we know about the car nothing's going to happen."

She didn't appear to hear me.

"Noel," she said quietly, "my husband, he's one of the men trying to find the diamonds, isn't he?" She reached out to grip Inahara's wrist. "Isn't he? Please—I want the truth."

For the first time since we'd met him, Inahara seemed uneasy. He stared at the tablecloth before answering her.

"Yes, Mrs Webster. I am afraid he is. In an endeavour to prevent you from delving into your husband's business too deeply, the embassy in London tried to persuade you that he had died in an aircraft which disappeared near Palau. I am aware that one of my colleagues bungled the job for which you must believe I am truly sorry."

"The press cutting," Lynne whispered. "Was Noel on the plane?"

"I don't know. Mrs Webster. There is still much I do not understand."

"But you know most of it," John said. "And now there's no bloody way any of us can get out of this deal even if we want to, is there?"

He sounded bitter — perhaps on Lynne's behalf or maybe for some reason of his own which I couldn't figure out. I was pretty sure he wasn't frightened and I didn't believe he was trying to deliberately antagonise Inahara but there was definitely something bothering him.

"Do you wish to get out, as you put it, Mr Hyland?"

"No, I'd have given the whole thing away before now if I did, but there's something we'd better get out in the open."

"Of course."

John glanced at me before he spoke again. "If you knew what you were up against, why not warn Daniel's brother-in-law, why not tell Lynne the truth in England and why ask Daniel and me to help the Japanese Government do their own salvage job?"

A smile hovered on Inahara's lips. "Firstly, Mr Hyland, what I have told you this evening is not something to be told to everyone. That is why Mr Hamill and Mrs Webster were not fully informed." His expression changed to one of seriousness. "Also I am at fault in not forseeing the extent of the danger. I regret I underestimated the lengths men are prepared to go to for such a large quantity of diamonds.

The second part of your question is more easily answered. You and Mr Chase were chosen simply because you are considered to be the best men in your particular fields. That you are not Japanese is of no consequence."

"So you were going to make us an offer to find the sub?" I said.

"No, Mr Chase. I would not have required Mr Hyland for that. I wish to make you an offer to find the aircraft. The diamonds are almost certainly no longer on board the submarine."

I checked my watch. "Okay," I said. "I think I
understand it all. What do we do now?"

Inahara caught the waiter's eye and asked him for the
bill.

"With Mrs Webster's permission we will omit our dessert
and coffee," he said. "It is wise for us to leave as soon as
possible. Before we do so, however, would you inspect
these?"

He placed two sheets of paper on the table, one in front
of John, the other for me.

I read mine through twice. When I glanced up John was
staring at me uncertainly, holding Inahara's pen in his
hand. "Jesus," he said quietly.

Inahara was waiting.

"What about Mrs Webster?" I asked.

"Although, as the wife of Noel Webster, I would prefer
that she return to England, she may accompany you at her
own expense if you insist."

I nodded at John waiting for him to scribble his
signature before he passed the pen across to me.

Then, for two thousand American dollars a day, plus all
travelling and living expenses, I too signed my soul over to
the Japanese Government.

"Does this mean you're not going to help me?" Lynne
remarked acidly. "I assume I've been out-bid."

"No," John said. "It means we're going out to Palau
together to find the plane and that means we'll find out
what the hell's been going on out there. It's what we were
going to do, anyway."

The strain was telling on her. I only hoped she'd hang
on long enough for us to get established somewhere so as
things could settle down a bit. As John had said, it'd be too
dangerous for her to return to London alone and, strangely,
I felt responsible for her.

Watching her as Inahara gathered up his contracts and
rose to his feet she seemed to take a grip on herself.

"I am sorry, Mrs Webster," he said. "You understand it is a job."

He paid the bill, pocketed the rubber band, the thread and the pencil and suggested we should leave the restaurant.

The girl was waiting for us at the door. Inahara spoke a few words to her then turned to me. "You have a cigarette, Mr Chase?"

"Yes, why?"

"I will show you in a moment. Please lead the way to your car."

For all I knew some bright bastard could gun the four of us down as we walked along the bank of the canal but we reached the Chevrolet without incident. I thought I was getting nervous again.

"Your key, Mr Hyland," Inahara requested.

John passed it to him without comment. Like me, I think, John realised he was probably in a class of his own as far as this sort of thing was concerned. He was completely confident in his approach to the car.

Opening the door without hesitation he inserted the key in the ignition switch and studied the instrument panel for a moment.

Taking the key out again he began using the thread to lash the pencil across its head forming an exaggerated handle in the shape of a T.

To one end of the pencil he fastened the rubber band and on the other he tied about eighteen inches of thread.

"Mr Chase, please remove any necessary luggage from the car. There is no danger providing you neither operate the bonnet catch nor try to start the engine. Then, if you would be so kind, the cigarette. Please light it before you give it to me."

I did as he asked, passing out Lynne's suitcase and the two bags John and I were carrying with us whilst I tried to figure out what the hell he was up to.

Using the point of the pencil he punched a neat hole

right through the cigarette I gave him twisting the thread through afterwards.

Suddenly I understood. I'd heard of cigarette fuses but I couldn't see how this one was going to operate. Until a second ago I hadn't even realised he intended to trigger the bomb but, now I thought about it, there was no point in some innocent employee from the rental company getting his head blown off when the car was finally located.

I watched Inahara closely, admiring the dexterity of his big hands as he worked.

Replacing the key in the ignition he tightened the thread with the smouldering cigarette dangling from it before securing its end to one of the knobs protruding from the instrument panel.

Now, for as long as the thread remained taut between the pencil and the knob, it would be impossible for the key to rotate in the lock.

Next, with the utmost delicacy, he strained the rubber band from the other end of the pencil to another convenient knob — and the job was finished.

It was so simple and so bloody clever. When the cigarette eventually burned through the thread, the rubber band would immediately exert sufficient force on the end of the pencil to turn the key. A fuse which had cost nothing and one which could hardly fail to work.

When Inahara turned round, the concentration still showed in his eyes. "Mr Chase, you could have observed from a distance."

"If I'd thought you were about to blow yourself up, I would have," I said. "You've done that a few times before, haven't you?"

He didn't answer me, indicating instead that we should retire to a safe distance from the car.

"I trust there are no people nearby?" he inquired.

"No," John said. "There're some cars parked along there, though."

"Ah, but the owners will have them insured, Mr Hyland. There are difficulties or complications only when the owners themselves are destroyed."

Lynne looked sideways at me and slid her arm into mine. It was a slightly familiar gesture and I wasn't sure if she was frightened of the impending bang or whether she wanted reassurance after the rather casual way Inahara had referred to the destruction which was about to take place.

A hundred yards away the four of us waited in a group beside the silent canal. I had a vision of my cigarette swinging gently on that single vital thread.

And then the night erupted in one huge sheet of orange fire. Pieces of car shot upwards to crash down again long after the roar of the explosion had died away and the initial brightness gradually gave way to white flame.

I felt Lynne shudder. "It could've been us," she breathed. "My God, what have we got mixed up in?"

Ripples on the surface of the canal caused by falling wreckage made the reflection of the burning car swim towards us where we stood. I watched them, thinking of Gerry, thinking of Jean and knowing beyond all doubt that things were certainly not the same as they'd been two evenings ago when I'd stepped off the plane.

People were starting to gather in the street and I could hear the wail of a distant siren.

As if by command, a taxi drew alongside us. Inahara opened a door and began loading our cases, John helping him with the last one.

"Time to go," Inahara said curtly with a glance at his watch. "Our flight leaves in less than half an hour."

Wordlessly I helped Lynne into the car knowing, as she did, that there was no point in arguing or in asking questions. I was sure we all knew where we were going.

As I climbed in after her and closed the door I caught sight of the driver. I was not surprised to recognise the boyfriend of our guardian angel.

SIX

There are two ways to fly from Hawaii to Guam. One of them is a glorious island-hopping adventure across nearly four thousand miles of ocean, the other is a lot faster and nothing like as interesting. Not surprisingly, Inahara had booked us on the fast one.

We'd been driven directly to the Honolulu air terminal to board a TWA jet just before midnight and now, less than an hour later, we were well on our way on a non-stop transpacific flight to Guam.

Watching the lights of Honolulu drop behind us after take-off, I'd remembered the other times I'd made this trip on the 727s of Air Micronesia bound for one of the outlying islands on some crazy money spinning job. Kwajalein, Majuro, Ponape—I had memories of them all and even some of Guam itself, but Palau was somewhere I'd never been before.

Our departure from Hawaii had been so hurried that I was suffering from the same vague feeling of unreality I'd experienced several times lately. I was not accustomed to exploding cars, strange Japanese bomb disposal experts nor an income of two thousand dollars a day. Incredibly, the whole thing had taken place in the last forty eight hours and I was conscious of a growing tiredness.

In the seat beside me Lynne had already fallen asleep, her long dark hair draped across her face as though she had arranged it purposely. The pillow I'd given to her lay unused on her lap and her breathing was deep and regular. I hoped she'd stay asleep for a while. On a long flight like this there would be too long to think and I knew she was all thought out.

She'd had no opportunity to rest, shower or change her clothes and, since her arrival in Honolulu, Lynne Webster had probably had to face up to more unpleasantness than she'd encountered in the whole of her life before. I felt sorry for her.

Ahead of me, on the next row of seats, John and Inahara were talking in undertones with John occasionally drawing on a pad of TWA writing paper he'd laid out on the table in front of him.

I leaned forward to find out what was going on.

"Have you put the lady to bed?" John asked.

"She didn't need any help from me. What am I missing back here?"

Inahara pointed to a diagram John had drawn. "Mr Hyland is giving a short lecture on trailing vortex turbulence, or TVT as I have learned it is called."

"For the kind of dough this job pays I'll lecture on anything you like," John grinned. "Just name your subject."

"I'll listen," I said, "but only to your TVT course, thanks. Have I missed much?"

"Not really. I'll start again, anyway." He took a clean sheet of paper and sketched an excellent illustration of a Boeing 707 in the top left-hand corner. Trailing from each wing tip, parallel with the fuselage, he drew a long narrow cone extending across the entire page. Then, using the side of his pencil lead, he shaded two wide spirals curving outwards from the exhausts of each engine to coil around the cones.

"Okay," he said. "Now, in the wake of every large aircraft you get paired vortexes formed aerodynamically by the wings. Air deflected upwards by the leading edge of each wing establishes a boundary layer which separates from the wing surface and rolls itself up into a spiral vortex like this one." He pointed to one of the shaded spirals he'd drawn.

"No matter how many engines are providing thrust, once you get a reasonable way behind the aircraft a dominant pattern forms. The end result is a pair of vortex cores separated by a distance roughly equal to the aircraft's wingspan. These cores aren't very large in diameter — usually no more than three percent of the wingspan, but on a 747 or a DC10 they're still perfectly intact fifteen miles behind the plane and they're still spinning."

"And it's these cores that are dangerous?" I asked.

"You bet your life they are. You've got air spiralling round at maybe two hundred miles an hour and if you fly into one of these babies in a light aircraft you're in real trouble. Between the two cores there's an induced downwash but outside them the turbulence acts in an upward direction. Either way they'll throw a small plane around like it was made of paper."

Inahara appeared deeply interested. "It really is possible to calculate the exact effect of this on a following plane, Mr Hyland?"

John shook his head. "No, it's not. Even a computer doesn't help much. But if you've done enough work on these things and if you've got actual experience on what happens under flight conditions you can use some clever mathematics to help you make a damned good guess. As long as someone's got data on the weather and we can get hold of the flight paths for those two planes, I can probably do enough work to get close."

"Closer than anyone else?" I said. "Or is there a chance our opposition could have hired themselves a tame expert who could give them the same sort of information?"

"There were a couple of other guys in NASA at the AMES Research Centre who might still be working on the project. But I know the emphasis has been changed to find out methods of breaking up the vortexes. I don't think anyone else has got the same sort of practical background that I've had."

"And so we have the edge," Inahara commented with obvious satisfaction. "With your underwater experience, Mr Chase, I am confident we will find the aircraft first."

"Do you really believe we're in a race?" I asked.

He nodded. "The opposition are desperate to buy time. With you and Mr Hyland working on the search, they must know we are well placed to win."

John was doodling a skull and crossbones on his sheet of paper.

"How the hell do they know though, Inahara?" he asked.

The Japanese spread his hands. "Someone in my embassy is certainly being paid to leak confidential information. He will be found and punished."

"Maybe you should've started looking for him earlier," I said. "Then Gerry might still be alive."

Inahara turned sideways in his seat. "I have said he will be found. I did not say how long the search has been going on. We have known of the problem for several months but until recently the informant had not interfered with my project."

I didn't push it. It couldn't help Gerry and I had no wish to stir up unnecessary trouble. As it was more than likely that we'd all be living in each others pockets during the next few days or weeks, I knew it was important to start establishing a good working relationship as early as possible. If the aircraft was lying in water deep enough to require me to use air pumped from the surface, I wanted to be sure of the men looking after my life support systems. They didn't have to be friends but it helped to have people with just a bit more than a financial interest in what I was doing, no matter how enormous the interest might be.

"Have you already made arrangements for us in Palau?" I asked. "Or are we playing the whole thing by ear as we go along?"

"Experience has taught me that it is better to formulate plans as occasion demands, Mr Chase," Inahara replied.

"Providing one has sufficient funds, it is better to proceed in whichever direction is the most promising whilst being ready to abandon any dead ends the moment they are found to be profitless."

"So what do we do first?" John inquired.

"Ah, Mr Hyland, you are impatient to begin. I share your enthusiasm. On arrival in Guam we will proceed to Agana where hotel reservations have been made for us. There, all the available data on the two aircraft will be waiting together with what I hope will be sufficient equipment for you to complete your initial analysis."

"What equipment?"

"Two programmable desk calculators, a digital x-y plotter and copies of the most detailed maps of the area which are known to exist. I was advised you would require these things."

John grinned at him. "I might—but I hope I can figure out an answer using a fifty dollar pocket calculator in a couple of days."

"Maybe you ought to spin it out a bit," I said. "If you make it three days that's an extra two thousand bucks."

I'd made the remark deliberately to try Inahara out. It didn't work. Instead of the serious frown I'd expected there was a broad smile. Perhaps he wasn't all machine after all.

"There is a bonus for speed, gentlemen," he said. "I did not mention it before. Today is Saturday, October the twenty third—providing the diamonds are in my hands within two weeks, for each day you have worked you will receive an additional payment of five hundred dollars."

I made a rapid mental calculation. Fourteen days at two and a half thousand a day was thirty five thousand dollars for me and the same for John. With the expenses and the cost of the diving equipment I'd need, this little operation was going to cost the Japanese Government the best part of a hundred thousand.

"I'll want some pretty complicated gear," I said. "Unless the plane's in shallow water in which case you mightn't need me at all."

"I have arranged for full deep sea equipment operating on a warm mixture of helium and oxygen," Inahara said. "There will also be the necessary lights and the best American decompression facilities should you be using scuba equipment. You must understand that I am paid to make certain we are successful."

By now I understood very well indeed. With four million dollars at stake, a few hundred thousand one way or the other was chicken feed. The Japanese weren't skimping on anything.

I lay back in my seat to wonder about Inahara for the hundredth time. Someone had entrusted him with this whole project, as he called it, and whoever had done the choosing must have known Inahara's track record. I guessed our grizzled Japanese friend had done this sort of thing a few times before and I was pretty sure he was damned good at it.

Gently I slid the pillow under Lynne's head and pulled the hair away from her face. Then I closed my eyes and let myself sink into a sleep I'd been looking forward to for a long time now.

Six and a half hours later I woke up with a throat like sandpaper and a craving for food and drink. Everyone else on board seemed to have been awake for quite a while. There was a buzz of conversation, the inevitable queue for the toilet and a general air of anticipation among the passengers.

I inspected my watch. Our flight time was supposed to be seven hours forty minutes so we were nearly there.

Lynne wasn't in her seat.

A passing hostess stopped to inquire if I was alright and if I needed anything.

"A cold beer, please," I said to her. "And, if it's not too much trouble, a thick American red beef sandwich."

"I can get one fixed for you," she said smiling. "How about some coffee instead of the beer? It's fresh, I've just made it."

"That'll be fine. Have you got anything else that might wake me up?"

She twisted the fresh air nozzle wide open and directed it at my face. "Black coffee," she said firmly. "I know the feeling, though. See how you are after a couple of cups."

I stood up and lit a cigarette. It tasted terrible.

From memory, Guam was ten hours ahead of Greenwich and I knew Hawaii was ten hours behind so, after nearly eight hours in the air, it should be around four o'clock in the morning when we got off the plane.

John and Inahara were both drinking coffee whilst studying a large coloured map of Micronesia they'd found from somewhere. John looked as lousy as I felt.

"Ah, Mr Chase," Inahara said. "You have slept well?"

"The sleep was great," I said. "It's the waking up bit that's not so hot."

"Yes, indeed. You must have been extremely tired — please try one of these." He reached in his pocket and passed me a small glass tube of white tablets.

"Benzadrine?" I inquired.

"If you would prefer not to." He held out his hand.

I took one of the pills and swallowed it before I gave him back the tube. "Thanks — where's Mrs Webster?"

"She's having breakfast down the back somewhere," John said. "She's going to be okay, Daniel. She looked a hell of a lot better after she'd taken one of Inahara's wake up pills." He grinned at me. "I've been doing some thinking. You know, if we pull this one off we'd make a hell of a good team for aircraft salvage."

"Wait and see," I growled, in no mood for considering anything that far ahead. "Let's find this one first."

Lynne and the hostess returned together. I let Lynne into her seat and took the tray with my drink and sandwich on it.

"Goodmorning, Daniel," she said. "I'm sorry if I woke you up getting out. There's not much room I'm afraid."

"You didn't," I said. "I was dead to the world. I only woke up because I've got one of those clocks inside me that automatically tells me when we're about to land."

As I finished speaking the seat belt and no smoking sign came on. Putting out my cigarette I attacked the sandwich, washing it down with mouthfuls of coffee whilst I watched out the window for the lights on the ground.

This time the old feeling was there alright. Maybe it was the pill or maybe it was because I'd got myself tied up in this weird hunt for Inahara's diamonds. Whatever the reason — it was back.

Like an old friend I waited for the tingling sensation to crawl up my spine as the dots of light drew closer and became more numerous on our approach to Guam International.

Our captain put us down beautifully on a pair of cushioned rails, turning the nose of the plane as soon as he'd stopped braking to taxi over to the floodlit terminal building.

Outside on the tarmac it was much hotter than it had been in Honolulu but it was nice to be breathing real fresh air again. We followed Inahara through the building directly to the carpark where we waited whilst he went over to speak to a neatly dressed man whom I presumed had been waiting for us to arrive.

When Inahara rejoined us he was frowning. "Another party of men arrived her late yesterday," he said. "They checked through a large quantity of airfreighted diving equipment in the cargo area here a few hours ago and have arranged to have it forwarded to Palau by special charter flight."

"When does my gear get here?" I asked him.

"It has been directed straight to Koror on Palau, Mr Chase. I trust it will be waiting for us when we reach there."

"You must've been damned sure I'd bite."

"Fairly sure, but in case you did not I had two substitutes standing by, Mr Chase. Neither, however, were nearly as suitably qualified as you are."

Lynne smiled at me. "You might as well stop asking him that sort of question, Daniel. He's been planning this much longer than any of us."

Inahara took John's case. "I would be grateful if you would drive us to Agana, Mr Hyland. It is not far and I will direct you. My colleague has already checked our car thoroughly for us."

This time we were to travel in class. A late model white Mercedes pulled up beside us driven by the neatly dressed man who had met us. He climbed out, showed Inahara a slim wooden box which was resting on the back seat then shook hands without speaking and walked away into the shadows of the car park.

I stowed our luggage in the boot before joining Inahara in the back of the car. He was busy unpacking his box.

"Just follow the sign posts, Mr Hyland," he instructed. "We will join the correct road shortly after we have cleared the vicinity of the airport."

Once the artificiality created by the lights and concrete of the terminal had been left behind we headed towards the west coast of the island driving through a soft still night with the familiar smell of jungle and savannah pouring in through the open windows.

Ten minutes later Inahara leaned forward to speak to John.

"I regret I have been told that we will almost certainly be apprehended somewhere on the road to Agana," he said calmly.

This was something I hadn't anticipated. I wasn't even sure I heard him properly.

"Please follow my instructions absolutely should you observe anything unusual, Mr Hyland. Mrs Webster, it will be advisable for you to kneel on the floor in the event of unpleasantness."

"Christ, Inahara," I said angrily. "We could've waited until daylight or gone another way or something. What the hell's the rush?"

"You are frightened, Mr Chase?"

"No," I shouted, "I'm just bloody annoyed. This isn't a war and it's not some sort of game either. What about Lynne?"

"I have explained before that time is short. You are entirely correct in stating that this is not a game. It is a fight, Mr Chase, with millions of dollars for the winner. You must remember Mrs Webster is here by choice and you must start to understand what you are being paid for."

He handed me something from the box on the floor. Cool, smooth and oily it slipped naturally into my hand. Without needing to look I knew what it was. It'd been a long time since I'd held one of these but I could even recognise the model just from the way it felt.

"The safety is by your thumb," Inahara said, "and the magazine is in place. The breech, however, is at present empty."

It hadn't been hard for John to guess what was going on.

"Can you use one of those, Daniel?" he asked over his shoulder.

"I can," I replied grimly, "but I hadn't planned on it."

Inahara lifted something else out of the box. In the dark I couldn't see it very well but the outline was enough to tell me he was assembling a small sub-machine gun. I heard him snap the pieces together.

The gradual realisation of what might happen was making the butt of the P38 Walther grow sticky in my hand.

Lynne hadn't said a word since Inahara had mentioned the possibility of an ambush. Now she swung round to address him.

"We've only just arrived—how can they know we're here or where we're going? How can they?" she sounded scared.

"No doubt by precisely the same means we have employed to discover their plans, Mrs Webster."

Even before she asked it I knew what her next question was going to be.

"It could be my husband who's waiting for us, couldn't it?" she said, her voice sinking. "He may even know I'm in the car."

"Inahara," John shouted urgently. "Quick."

A quarter of a mile ahead of us, illuminated in our headlight beams, a long row of oil drums had appeared.

Guarding what looked like a large excavation extending across more than half the width of the road, they'd been carefully arranged to force all traffic partly onto the gravel verge.

I hadn't the slightest doubt what they were for and now I was really frightened.

Flickering yellow lights on the top of each drum revealed nothing but a yellow clay bank flanking one side of the road, a road repair sign and a battered truck parked on the grass beside the supposed excavation.

Slowing the car to a crawl as we drew closer, John waited silently for his instructions. I wondered if he was frightened, too.

"Get on the floor, Lynne," I said. "Don't kneel down, lie down if you can."

I wound down my window then pulled back the slide on the Walther and let it snap shut. I thought I was probably as ready as I ever would be.

Inahara was still peering intently ahead trying to make up his mind. There wasn't much time left.

"Mr Hyland, I have made my decision. Please accelerate

as rapidly as you can and head directly for the drums. On no account attempt to drive on the section of the road which they wish us to use. This is a very strong motor car and we will have to hope the drums have not been filled with water or concrete."

He opened his window and prepared himself for action.

There were a few seconds for me to rationalise Inahara's decision and just time to wonder if part of the road had really been mined before the sudden glare of headlights from the truck signalled the beginning of it all.

Inahara didn't wait to find out if he had assessed the situation correctly. Fifty yards from the roadblock he fired two short bursts, killing one of the lights on the truck.

Instantaneously his fire was returned and I heard the angry spatter of lead on the road beside me.

Still gaining speed, at forty miles an hour, John lined the Mercedes up with the gap between the nearest pair of drums.

As we smashed into the first one, Inahara's third burst shot out the remaining headlight.

Red flashes stabbed out of the darkness towards me.

Mercifully the drums were empty. Cannoning off our battered front mudguards like giant skittles, I could feel the impact from each one of them and I knew the whole front end of the Mercedes was taking a hell of a beating.

The Walther bucked steadily in my hand as I pumped out bullet after bullet in the direction of the flashes, waiting fatalistically for that first agonising bite of pain to tell me some bastard out there had made a lucky shot.

The noise was indescribable and the inside of the car was filled with smoke and empty cartridges flying from Inahara's sub-machine gun.

His lights gone long ago, John was fighting a losing battle against the drums, each successive collision slowing the Mercedes by several miles an hour.

Then, as suddenly as it had begun, it was all over.

Lynne was sobbing on the floor and I could hear John swearing in one long non-stop effort to contain his feelings.

As far as I could tell, I seemed to be okay.

"Inahara," I said. "Are you alright?"

I saw a gleam of teeth in the dark patch which was his face.

"Of course, Mr Chase. It sounds as though Mr Hyland and Mrs Webster are also unhurt."

For the next minute none of us said anything, leaving John to carry on driving through the darkness. Considering he couldn't see where he was going, I thought he was doing a hell of a good job.

"The radiator," John said eventually. "If it's still got water in it I want a medal for defensive driving."

"Never mind the radiator water, have you still got yours?" I asked him in a faint attempt at humour.

"Yeah, but next time you can drive Daniel. You're older than I am. You haven't got so long to go." He reached out a hand to help Lynne back onto her seat.

She came up with cartridge cases in her hair.

"You're all mad," she said. "Crazy mad."

"Are you okay?" I asked.

She'd stopped the quiet crying but when I put my hand on her shoulder I could feel her trembling. I remembered she'd been like this back in Honolulu when the Chev had exploded.

"Yes, I think so. I was just terrified. It was horrible, I'm still shaking now."

"Mrs Webster," Inahara said, "I can assure you that you were not alone in your fright. I have been shot at on numerous occasions but I am always frightened. If it happens again tomorrow I will find it similarly unnerving."

Christ, I thought — unnerving. An understatement even for Inahara. I lit a cigarette watching him pass Lynne something from his magic box.

"Mrs Webster, if you hold this out of the window and

direct the beam at the edge of the road it will assist Mr Hyland."

It was a powerful flashlight and although a poor substitute for headlights it was a hell of a lot better than nothing at all. With its aid, John managed to keep the sick Mercedes going at about thirty miles an hour for the remainder of the journey with only a couple of minor excursions off the road.

Agana was no more than a few miles from the airport and we arrived in town shortly before the radiator ran completely dry. With steam hissing out everywhere beneath the bonnet; Inahara directed us to our hotel where we parked what was left of the car and unloaded our luggage.

I don't know whether it was plain curiosity which made me hang back as the others made their way to the hotel entrance or whether something far more complicated was at work inside my head.

Using the flashlight Lynne had given to me I carefully explored the bodywork of the Mercedes for bullet holes. Destruction from the drums had been pretty savage but, try as I might, I couldn't find a single puncture in the metal anywhere.

In itself, I suppose, that was not so very extraordinary. We'd been moving fairly fast and there hadn't been much light. It was when I made my second inspection several hours later in the daylight that everything suddenly took one enormous lurch sideways.

Randomly spaced along each side of the car, I counted at least twenty neat round holes which certainly hadn't been there the first time I'd looked.

SEVEN

Bright sunshine filled the whole room and far away to the north, through the open window, I could see the white line of surf frothing on Ipao beach.

Looking much like any other American resort in the Pacific, Agana was laid out below us, its houses and hotels grouped in clumps between the dark green vegetation. Only one of Guam's ancient columns of coral rock standing alone beside one of the parks I could see served to remind me where we were.

With his back to the view, John sat behind a desk so littered with paper that it was difficult to understand how he had managed to create such an incredible mess in such a short time. He wore a pair of stereo earphones and had been busy punching away at one of his calculators when I first entered the room.

I picked up a piece of paper which had blown off his desk. Both sides of it were covered with columns of figures written in untidy ballpoint. Folding it into a dart I threw it at him.

He didn't even bother to look up when it skimmed across the desk to make a graceful landing near his telephone.

Lighting a cigarette, I took a seat and waited.

A moment later he put down his pen but kept his head bent forwards as if studying something he'd written. I knew damned well he wasn't because his eyes were shut but I didn't interrupt in case he was immersed in thought. I needn't have worried.

Three or four minutes later he pulled off the earphones

and grinned at me. "Tchaikovsky," he announced. "Bloody marvellous."

"I thought you were working," I said caustically. "How the hell are we going to find the plane if you sit around listening to music all day long?"

His grin broadened. He picked up my dart, unfolding it and smoothing it flat before carefully dropping it back onto the floor.

"Ah, Mr Chase," he said in a passable imitation of Inahara. "You must understand that different people have different methods of solving problems. If I choose to listen to classical music whilst undertaking this onerous task, that is my business. You will agree it is the results which matter —not the method used to obtain them."

"Horseshit," I said. "What results?"

He stood up and ran his fingers through his hair. "Daniel, my friend, you're a lousy disbeliever. If you play bagpipes underwater when you're trying to find Inahara's boxes of diamonds you can count on my complete understanding." He pointed to what had been my dart and to half a dozen other sheets of paper scattered about the floor. "With the assistance of Tchaikovsky and with my extraordinary talent I am nearly there."

Leaving my cigarette in the ashtray I collected the papers from the floor and inspected them closely. Differential calculus has never been my best subject and the mathematics smothering each sheet was utterly meaningless to me.

John took them, stapled them together and dropped the bundle into one of the desk drawers. 'Tomorrow," he said, "or even tonight if I don't make any more mistakes. Right now I need lunch. How about you?"

"I want to know why you chuck your answers on the floor and leave all the stuff that's no good on the desk."

"Much quicker, Daniel. Once it's on the floor you can't lose it underneath a lot of other junk. Stop criticising my system. Come on, let's go and get outside a cold beer. I'll tell you how far I've got when I've unwound."

"Okay," I said. "But before we go there's something I want to ask you."

"What's that?"

"Last night—or earlier this morning during our exciting little drive from the airport; how many people do you reckon were out there in the dark?"

"Christ, I don't know—I wasn't counting. Why?"

"I just wondered what we're really up against. I don't know if we're outnumbered and it might be useful to get some idea—that's all."

Without having to drop any hints on my recent discovery, I wanted him to talk about the attack on the car. Whilst there was absolutely no reason to suspect John of anything, I'd decided to play things very close to my chest from now on. Something very peculiar was going on and, until I found out what it was, I had no intention of confiding in John Hyland or anyone else.

Since stumbling accidentally on the artificial bullet holes, I'd been trying to think of a rational explanation for them, but I knew damn well there could really only be one. For some reason or other, someone had gone to an awful lot of trouble to fake the whole incident which had occurred on the road to Agana. And that raised so many other questions it was hard to know where to even begin thinking about the project we were supposed to be working on.

"Judging on the muzzle flashes, I'd say there were about five guns," John said. "I was a bit busy to see properly."

"Lucky they missed the windshield," I said. "And us, too."

"Yeah. I thought about that afterwards. I don't see how the hell we got away with it. They hit the car all along both sides. Did you see the holes?"

I nodded. "Maybe this is going to be one of those lucky jobs. I've been on some before. Keep your fingers crossed."

John grinned again. "You can look at that two ways. We weren't that lucky being caught driving a white car, were we?"

I hadn't thought of that before. Pure coincidence or deliberately arranged? For two pins I'd have told John what I knew but something was still telling me to wait until I was certain. There was no hurry yet and I had a strong feeling it was important not to make a mistake.

"Lunch," John said walking to the door. "Maybe some bastard will have a go at us in the daylight where we can see him."

"Somehow I don't think they will," I said.

The hotel Inahara had chosen for us was not located in central Agana but perched on a steep hillside overlooking the downtown area facing out to sea. As well as the main dining room, on the ground floor there were two pleasant open air bars, one of them with tables overflowing out onto a small terrace surrounded by shrubs and trees. We chose a table in an empty corner of the outside section and ordered salads and some American beer.

"Do you know where Lynne is?" John asked.

"Still in her room as far as I know. She was pretty upset."

"Might've been better if she hadn't taken that pill Inahara gave her," John said. "Then she could've got some more sleep. Even though she crashed out on the plane, another few hours could've helped with the shock."

"What do you really think of her?" I asked.

He shrugged. "I can understand her wanting to find her husband. At least I think I can. But I figure we were probably stupid bringing her with us—specially now we know what the score is."

"If we do know," I said quietly.

He gave me a tight lipped smile. "Don't think you're alone in that, old buddy. Twenty five hundred bucks a day makes me wonder about Inahara's diamonds a whole lot more than you might think."

Our conversation was interrupted by the arrival of our waiter. After he'd gone John seemed unwilling to elaborate on his last remark. Instead he started pencilling a map on the formica table top.

Beside my plate he drew an ellipse with the letter G inside it. "Guam," he explained. On the other side of the table he drew a second ellipse with a number of dots at one end of it. "And that's Palau."

Not to be outdone, I dipped my finger in my beer and traced a wet line between the two islands. Half way along it I placed an olive from my salad.

"Yap," I said. "Now you know my geography's as good as yours."

"Fine," John said. "What you've drawn is more or less the flight route of the 727 that was supposed to have been in the air when the other plane went missing. I've got its departure time, its rate of climb and all the weather data. Inahara even managed to steal a copy of the flight log from somewhere, so I've got that too."

"What about the plane we're interested in?"

"Not so good—I mean as far as data's concerned. Don't forget it was a private aircraft and way out here sometimes the regulations aren't enforced too well. One interesting thing that's got nothing to do with my calculations is the fact that there's no record of who was on board—not even the pilot's name."

"Surprise," I said dryly. "Don't tell Lynne, she'll really start believing her husband's alive."

John grinned. "If he turns out to be one of those guys who shot at me last night, for her sake I hope he's already dead."

"Tell me about the plane," I said.

He took a scrap of paper from the pocket of his shirt and read from it. "A nineteen seventy two Piper Aztec, number H 5316 S, registered in Manila for private charter work. Five seats and a pair of two hundred and fifty horsepower Lycoming engines."

"How well do you know the type of aircraft?"

John took a long drink of beer before answering. "Flown a couple of them. They probably rate as one of the most docile low wing twins in the world. Their top speed's over two hundred but they've got a real thick, short wing section and that means they're very safe at low airspeeds."

"So the pilot was unlucky if the vortex cores made him lose control?"

John shook his head. "Not really. An Aztec has a gross weight of about five thousand pounds, that's not much mass if it accidentally flew into a TVT from a 727 even though a 727 isn't all that big, either."

He began drawing more lines on the table.

"I know where the 727 was at any time after it left Palau on its way here, and I know roughly what time the Piper took off — about a quarter of an hour ahead of the Boeing. Inahara's got a statement from one eye witness that says the Piper didn't head straight off for Guam. I don't know why but, unless it was intending to land on Palau again, it'd have to have been heading for refuelling at Yap. A Piper Aztec carries about a hundred and forty gallons of gasoline and that'll only take it twelve hundred miles or so.

Anyway, taking a climb rate of fifteen hundred feet a minute I've done my calculations and I've figured out what would happen to a typical Aztec for two specific TVT conditions."

"Excellent, Mr Hyland." Inahara appeared beside us. Lynne was with him.

I stood up and found two more chairs for them.

Lynne stared at the mass of lines on the table top.

"Heavens," she said, "you should've sat at a larger table."

There was colour in her cheeks and she looked fresh and pretty. Wearing an attractive patterned, cotton dress and with her long hair tied back with a ribbon, the Lynne Webster of this afternoon was a very different person to the one I'd seen before. I was even conscious of the fact that she had an exceptionally good figure.

The cool aloofness I'd been aware of when I had first met her at Honolulu was not in evidence but she had regained her composure and the dullness had gone from her eyes. She sat beside me, smoothing down her dress and smiling slightly.

I nodded to the waiter.

Lynne ordered an omelette and a long gin and lemonade. Inahara said he'd already lunched in his room but that he'd be pleased to join us in a beer.

John was using a paper table napkin to clean his drawing board before starting again. This time he sketched a much larger map of the Palau District showing the location of the airport on the southern tip of the main island of Babelthuap. Further to the south he drew the outlines of Koror Island, some tiny circles to represent the Rock Islands and, at the very bottom of his picture, a larger island which he named Peleliu.

"There's another one called Angaur down there, too," he said. "But we won't worry about it. The 727 took off to the south then turned through three hundred and sixty degrees before heading off here to Guam. This is more or less its flight path—but don't forget its climbing all the time."

He drew a long hairpin on the table stretching it right out over the Rock Islands towards Peleliu.

"And here are two of the possible routes the Aztec could have taken—there's one more I haven't worked out yet." He added two more curved lines passing through the hairpin at different angles.

Inahara unclipped a pen from his shirt pocket and added small dots at the points where the lines crossed each other. He looked disappointed.

"Mr Hyland," he said. "Because the 727 flew back on itself as you have shown, there are two possible intersections for each flight path of the Piper Aztec, are there not?"

"Right."

"And there are three probable flight paths for the smaller aircraft?"

John grinned at him. "Right again—and you think that makes six places where the Aztec could've got fouled up in the vortexes."

I knew John wouldn't be so cocky if he really believed we were going to have to search the sea bed in six different locations. There was something he hadn't told us yet.

The waiter returned carrying Lynne's omelette and the drinks.

Inahara was visibly frustrated at the interruption, using his pen to enlarge the dots he'd drawn as if unable to believe our misfortune. To make it worse John excused himself for a moment and headed off to the toilet.

I used the pause to try and guess who amongst us was not what they seemed. It was a game I was going to become familiar with in the days which lay ahead.

Inahara was undoubtedly anxious to get his hands on the diamonds. Lynne Webster was surely equally anxious to locate her husband and John would have died from nerve gas if I hadn't rescued him on that first day back in Honolulu. Glancing at each of them in turn I could find no clue which might tell me what I wanted to know. Soon I'd have to start planting some seeds of my own to try and force the pace a little. If I left it too late I could easily find myself wandering around on the bottom of the Pacific with three people on the surface who might be quite happy to leave me there once their precious diamonds had been hauled up.

"Solved it yet?" John asked on his return.

"I have," Lynne announced brightly. "You've got to look sideways at the flight paths—not down on top of a map like the one you've drawn. If you imagine lines at an angle to the ground which represent the way the two aircraft climbed then you might find their flight paths never crossed at all. Is that right?"

"Exactly right," John smiled. "It's a three dimensional problem, not a two dimensional one. That's what makes it a bit tricky. It's even more difficult in practice because both planes climb in curves not in straight lines and I've got to work out the strength of the vortexes at all the places where the Aztec could have got near the TVT from the 727."

"Which is what you're getting paid for," I said cheerfully. "Stop upsetting our Japanese friend here."

Inahara permitted himself a smile. "I will wait until you have finished, Mr Hyland. I am sorry if I appeared too eager."

John drained his glass. "While Daniel and I are busy, just make sure nobody decides to shoot at us again. I'll go and draw some more of Lynne's sideways pictures," he smiled at her. "Daniel, if you've got nothing better to do, you could give me a hand."

I stood up and spoke to Lynne. "The sooner we get this bit done the sooner we'll get to Palau."

She looked up at me. "I know. I wish I could do something to help."

For a second there was something in those dark brown eyes which made me change my mind about her completely. I think I must have stared at her too long. She moved her eyes away and picked up her glass.

Following John back into the hotel I thought things had begun moving very rapidly indeed.

EIGHT

By eleven o'clock on Sunday evening I'd realised why John Hyland had been given a free ticket to fly out from Australia and I'd nearly begun to believe he was worth all the dollars Inahara was paying him. I mightn't know much about aeronautics but of one thing I had no doubt—the young man who'd been hired to discover where the Piper Aztec had crashed possessed one of the finest brains I'd ever come across.

After leaving Lynne and Inahara at the bar we'd gone straight to the room where John had been working earlier in the day. It was about two thirty when he'd started using his calculator again and for the next hour I'd done very little except gather up the pieces of paper he dropped on the carpet to make sure we didn't lose any of them.

Eventually he'd asked me whether I'd mind plotting a few graphs for him if he gave me the coordinates. Glad to be given something constructive to do I'd willingly followed his instructions, drawing the necessary axes on a number of sheets before beginning to fill in the points as he called them out.

When first starting the job I'd failed to appreciate John Hyland's extraordinary ability to think in three dimensions but very quickly learned of my mistake. In no time at all I'd found it necessary to pin my graphs on the walls so I could remember which one represented which dimension and to enable me to answer the stream of questions he fired at me as he made adjustments to his calculations.

In the end I wound up juggling with three flight paths

for the Piper Aztec drawn on nine separate sheets of graph paper and comparing them with six more sheets illustrating the hairpin path which the 727 had followed.

John was unwilling to stop for dinner and my stomach had been complaining about its diet of cigarette smoke for some hours when he'd finally put his arms round all of the papers on his desk to crumple them into one huge ball. That had been ten minutes ago.

On the floor the result of our labours lay before us. A single sheet of paper with two gently curving lines on it and a number of figures surrounding the point where the lines intersected.

Kneeling down John was still studying our master plan when there was a tap on the door.

"Come in," I said wearily.

Inahara stood outside, a bottle of champagne grasped in each huge hand. Behind him, carrying a large tray, Lynne was smiling at me through the haze of cigarette smoke drifting out into the corridor.

"Not food and drink," I said in mock astonishment. "I thought the idea was to starve us out until we produced the answer."

"And you have an answer, Mr Chase?" Inahara inquired, stepping into the room.

"Ask him," I said, pointing to John.

John rocked back on his heels but remained crouching. There was a broad grin on his face disguising the tiredness which had been there for the last few hours.

"Theme song," he announced. "The answer, my friend, is blowing in the wind; or, if you prefer it—swirling in the vortex." He held out our sheet of paper by one corner. Inahara exchanged it for one of his bottles.

Lynne was searching in vain for somewhere among the mess of paper to put down her tray.

"Anywhere you like except the floor," I said. "Would you believe the good stuff is only on the floor."

She moved John's giant ball of paper carefully to one side and placed the tray on his desk.

"We thought you'd probably have had enough," she explained. "We didn't think you'd finished, though. Do you know where to look now?"

John laughed at her. "We know where to look but whether anything's there is anybody's guess." He stood up and retrieved our best map of Palau from the corner of the room where I'd hurled it in disgust after discovering I'd drawn one of the graphs incorrectly.

"We'll have to use a sextant or something to actually pin point the place when we get there," he said. "But I can show you more or less if Inahara gives me back our results."

Inahara handed the sheet to him without saying a word.

John inspected his figures for a moment then used a pair of dividers to mark out the position on the map, something we hadn't done before.

Just south of Palau he drew a miniature picture of an aircraft and wrote the word treasure beside it in large letters.

We all gathered round to view the magic spot where the Aztec was supposed to have hit the water. I was particularly anxious to see whether I was going to have a deep water job to do.

Surrounding the whole of the Palau District, a wavy line indicating the limits of the coral reef defined what I guessed would be the rough boundary between deep and reasonably shallow water. Well outside the south-eastern edge of the reef, about one third of the way from Koror to the southern extremity of the Rock Islands, John had drawn his tiny plane.

"Mr Hyland," Inahara said. "Do you have need of this map?"

"No, have it with my compliments."

Inahara picked it up and glanced around the room. "I imagine you will require only the result sheet and the graphs with your coordinates on them?"

"That's right," John agreed. "Fifty pages of calculation for a few graphs—that's the way it is in this business."

"Mrs Webster, I would be grateful if you would assist me to clear up whilst Mr Chase and Mr Hyland eat a well deserved meal before it becomes cold. I am sure they must both be hungry."

We were indeed. John winked at me as we sat down to enjoy the food which Lynne had brought us. By the time we'd finished Inahara had collected a great sheaf of paper which he proceeded to stuff into a wastepaper bin using his foot to make sure none of it escaped. He placed the map on top of the pile.

I knew why he'd taken the bother and I knew it wasn't for reasons of tidiness.

"Now," he said cheerfully, "we will drink to our next success when Mr Chase finally confirms the position of the aircraft." He pulled a cork on one of the champagne bottles, his battered face wearing one of his special smiles reserved for occasions like this.

Like old friends the four of us shared two hotel glasses from the bathroom to drink a toast to ourselves. There was something incongruous about the way we were behaving. I was almost certain one or more of us must be putting on one hell of an act for the benefit of the others.

I lit a cigarette and drank three glasses of champagne in quick succession. Whilst I waited for it to work I studied Lynne Webster in close detail.

Wearing the same dress she'd had on at lunch she sat half facing me with an expression of relaxed pleasure on her face. She'd kicked off her sandals and untied the ribbon holding back her hair, letting it fall around her bare shoulders. Her earlier fears about her husband seemed to have vanished and I thought that perhaps, like me, the jolt of becoming involved in Inahara's crazy project had revitalised her in some peculiar way.

Then, almost before I knew what was happening, I felt myself become acutely aware of her nipples where they were pushing out against the fabric of her dress. For several minutes I was sure she knew I was staring at her.

She turned suddenly towards me. "Daniel, I know it's late and you're awfully tired but I'd love a walk in the fresh air. Would you mind?"

The champagne was fizzing in my head, the noise mixing with John's laughter at one of Inahara's remarks. At that very moment, as she stood up, I knew with great clarity that more than anything in the whole world I wanted to escort Lynne Webster to her room, tear off her clothes and take her straight to bed.

Inahara didn't let me answer. It was probably just as well.

"Mr Chase, before you and Mrs Webster leave I must tell you we are scheduled to leave for Palau at ten thirty tomorrow. It will be necessary for us to book out of here at approximately nine o'clock."

"One of these days you're going to jump the gun once too often and fall smack on your ugly face," John said good humouredly. "I could easily have taken another day, you know."

"Ah, but you didn't, Mr Hyland. Now, whilst Mr Chase and Mrs Webster go for their stroll, please be kind enough to stand by with one of the hotel fire extinguishers you will find in the corridor."

I rose to my feet just as John brushed by me.

He whispered in my ear. "Don't forget what happened last night, old buddy. It's dark out there."

Inahara had already set light to the contents of the wastepaper basket and smoke was beginning to pour out of the window. If the Agana fire brigade was called I wondered if they'd believe us if we told them truthfully what it was we were burning. Somehow I didn't think they would.

On the way downstairs with Lynne I mentioned that I considered it would be foolhardy to venture outside the hotel in the circumstances, then tried to convince myself she'd told me the truth about her reasons for going to Palau and enlistening my help in the first place. The exercise effectively dispelled my earlier feelings.

I said goodnight to her in the bar, ordered a double whisky to chase down the champagne and another one to chase away returning memories of Jean.

On Monday morning, October 25th, three and a half hours after leaving Guam airport, I sighted Palau for the first time. I certainly was not disappointed.

From two thousand feet Babelthuap, the largest island, was a magnificent black-green wilderness bordered by mangrove swamps and crystal clear water which covered the surrounding coral shelf. Beautiful jungle waterfalls slipped away under the aircraft's wheels as we lost altitude on our approach to the southern end of the island and with so much to watch I nearly forgot to look out for what I'd heard was one of the most spectacular sights in all the islands of the Pacific.

Squinting out of the window, I waited as the plane circled prior to landing.

And there, almost as far as I could see, a mass of tiny green islands swam into view like so many pin cushions floating on the ocean surface.

Lying in clusters, Palau's two hundred Rock Islands were a breathtaking sight. Extending for miles to the south, a labyrinth of winding channels was spread out in a random pattern among the green dots, islands and waterways merging together in the distance to form an unusual pale green horizon which was part land and part sea. I thought I should have come here before — long before.

Half lying across me as she strained for a better view, Lynne seemed equally impressed.

I could smell the freshness of her and her hand was warm where it rested on my arm. She was so close I could damn near taste her.

"It's wonderful," she said simply. "I've never seen anything like this, ever."

"There are some pretty special places out here if you know where to look," I said. "But this is as good as anything I've seen."

She pushed herself away from the window and prepared for our landing. "It's funny. All the days and weeks I've been imagining what it would be like—and now, after everything that's happened, I'm actually here." Her voice became quieter. "I'm glad I came, Daniel."

Picking up my bag from the floor I felt the hard bulge made by the Walther automatic and the wonder of the Rock Islands faded with the reminder of what I was here for.

Before we'd left Guam I'd checked three of the cartridges still remaining in the magazine, prising out the soft lead bullets to discover whether Inahara had tampered with them before giving me the gun. But all three had been fully charged with powder and perfectly capable of killing a man at normal handgun ranges.

Lying in bed last night I'd tried yet again to think of an explanation for the false bullet holes in the Mercedes, reviewing what I knew about John, Lynne and Inahara whilst searching for a flaw in one of their motives or perhaps hoping I'd remember something one of them had said which would give me a lead. I'd gone to sleep no further ahead than when I'd started and I was beginning to worry about my complete lack of progress.

Disembarking from the plane, Lynne linked her arm in mine as if it was the most natural thing in the world for her to do. It confirmed what I already knew. Pretty soon I'd have to decide what I was going to do about Mrs Webster for her sake and for mine, too.

Standing on the grass beside the runway Inahara waited for us to catch him up. "It is necessary for us to take the airport bus in order to reach Koror. We will also have to cross the waterway between Babelthuap and Koror by means of cable car. On arrival at our hotel, Mr Chase, you will be able to undertake a preliminary examination of your diving equipment."

"Do you reckon we'll get there in one piece?" I said. "The last time we got off a plane we only just reached the hotel and that was an ordinary road trip."

"I think we will find the action has moved further afield —if I may be permitted to use an American expression. I anticipate no further trouble until we are at sea, Mr Chase."

"Is that right," I answered, unable to suppress my sarcasm. "What makes you so sure?"

"Inscrutible oriental intuition," John said. "Either that or more guardian angels." The remark was made in such a way that Inahara could do no more than smile at it.

"Neither, Mr Hyland. Western logic tells me the rival organisation will know we have discovered the location of the aircraft simply by the fact that we have arrived here. Their failure to kill you when they had the opportunity means they knew we would beat them in their endeavour to find the sunken aircraft first. In their position what would you have done?"

"Wait for us to lead them to it?" Lynne suggested.

"Exactly, Mrs Webster. I regret to say we may anticipate serious opposition once Mr Chase is prepared to dive."

I thought that sounded very reassuring. I swore loudly to make certain everyone knew exactly how I felt about it.

NINE

It was gone midnight when the knock on my door dragged me out of a sodden sleep.

Rolling onto my side and squinting again at my watch I wondered if I'd imagined the noise. But no, there was another tap, slightly louder this time.

I climbed out of bed, fumbled with the switch on the bedside light and started searching for my clothes. Whilst it was hardly likely that anyone wanting to surprise me would bother to knock, I still preferred to greet whoever it was with my trousers on.

Narrowly avoiding serious injury by pulling up my zip too fast, I went to the door, wedged my foot firmly against it and turned the key in the the lock.

"Who is it?" I asked.

"Me, Lynne."

I let her in at once.

She was still fully dressed and didn't appear to have been to bed.

"I'm terribly sorry, Daniel. I hoped you mightn't have gone to sleep yet."

"That's okay. Come and have a drink."

I relocked the door behind her then went to sluice some cold water over my face.

After spending all afternoon and most of the evening breaking open wooden crates and checking over the diving equipment Inahara had ordered, I'd been dog tired when I'd eventually gone to bed. I must have been asleep for at least a couple of hours and Palau's sticky heat certainly wasn't helping me wake up.

She waited while I dried myself and searched for a cigarette.

Somehow I didn't think this was a social visit. I was too tired to be disappointed about it, although now I came to look at her more closely I wasn't quite so sure.

"There's some cold beer in the frig," I said. "I don't think I've got anything else, though."

"I don't want a drink, thank you. I just want to talk."

She sat down on the bed and stared at me with her extraordinary eyes. I still hadn't got used to them.

"What about?"

"This." She handed me an envelope.

"What is it?"

"Read it, Daniel."

I withdrew a grubby scrap of paper, holding it under the bedside lamp in order to see it better.

It began, Dearest Lynne, and I guessed who it was from immediately. The message was very simple.

> Meet me tonight on Babelthuap at the inlet just south of Airai. The boy will show you how to get here. For God's sake tell no-one of this.

It was signed Noel.

I was not as surprised as I thought I'd be. "There's no doubt about the handwriting I suppose?" I asked.

She shook her head. "None. You can check it against one of his other letters if you want, but I know it's Noel's writing."

I decided it was essential to have a beer. My brain was soggy and I couldn't think properly.

In the short time it took me to go to the kitchenette, open a can and return to the bedroom I'd convinced myself that Noel Webster really was alive and that this was the opportunity I'd been waiting for.

"When did you get the letter?" I said.

"A boy brought it to my room about ten minutes ago.

He's waiting for me outside the hotel. Apparently, at this time of night, the only way to get the the inlet is by boat. I suppose the cable car's closed."

"What about the bit that says for God's sake tell nobody?"

"You said you'd help me—remember?" Her eyes were pleading now.

"I remember. What do you want me to do?"

"Come with me, Daniel—please. I can't go by myself. I know he's my husband but I can't help being frightened."

Placing the half finished can of beer on the table, I stubbed out my cigarette and rummaged in the bag beside my bed for the Walther.

"Put on some sensible clothes and go and meet the boy downstairs. I'll follow you until you get to the boat. I'll be right behind you all the way. Don't get into the boat without me, though—if there's going to be an argument, that's where it'll start."

She got up, wrapped her arms around my neck and kissed me hard on the mouth. I was left standing in the room with the Walther hanging loosely in my hand. I felt rather stupid.

Why the hell she'd chosen a time like this to kiss me I couldn't imagine. Or, now she was about to be re-united with her husband, had it been nothing more than an impulsive way to say thank you? There wasn't time to think about it.

I slipped on my shoes, chose the darkest coloured shirt out of the three I had left and stuffed the gun into my trouser pocket.

The only other piece of equipment which might prove useful was the flashlight. I grabbed it, then, with the bedroom door ajar, waited for Lynne to appear in the corridor.

She wasn't long. Wearing a dark blue corduroy jacket and denim jeans, she trotted past a few minutes later heading for the stairs. I waited long enough for her to reach the lobby then let myself out and followed.

Lights from the hotel illuminated a small patch of lawn outside the front entrance but once away from the building it was pitch black. I didn't know whether a moonlit night would have suited my purpose better but a night as dark as this one certainly meant I'd have to stick pretty close to make sure I didn't lose Lynne on the way to the boat.

Accompanied by the smaller figure of what I imagined was one of the native Palau islanders, she'd been disappearing into the shadows as I arrived in the foyer. Walking as quietly as I could, I trailed them through a gap in the shrubs bordering the hotel grounds.

Despite a fairly vigorous night life, Koror, at gone midnight, was a very silent place indeed and, for the next three or four minutes I was hard pressed to keep them in sight without letting Lynne's guide know he was being followed.

Having had no chance to explore any of the surrounding area since our arrival on the island, I had only the vaguest idea of where we were headed but I did know there were a number of tidal creeks and some estuaries not far from the hotel. It seemed safe to assume the boat would be moored reasonably close by.

I'd travelled no more than half a mile along a narrow track or footpath when the vegetation suddenly opened out and the foreshore lay in front of me.

Only a short distance away, Lynne was standing on a clump of reeds whilst the islander dragged a small boat over the mud where the tide had left it stranded.

Taking advantage of the situation, I hurried forwards, my feet squelching into silt and mud of the estuary. I reached the reeds just ahead of the guide who had run back as soon as he'd heard me coming.

His English was rudimentary but understandable.

To save a lot of arguing I took the Walther from my pocket, showed it to him and put it away again.

Rather than appearing cowed or angry, he shrugged as if to indicate my arrival was not of his concern then trudged off through the mud to where the boat was floating in the shallows.

It was an extremely modest boat about nine feet long fitted with an equally modest outboard motor.

No sooner had we climbed aboard than I had to step out again to help push us over two sandbars before we were in water deep enough to tilt down the motor and start it. Even then, for some time afterwards, the propeller kept on kicking up mud from the bottom.

With Lynne perched in the bow the runabout was impossible to trim properly and, as it was far too tiny for the three of us to rearrange ourselves, it was necessary to keep the speed down to prevent even the smallest of bow waves from splashing into Lynne's lap.

At five or six knots we pulled steadily away from Koror leaving a wake almost as black as the land behind us.

Despite his diminutive stature, I judged our guide to be about nineteen years old. Well muscled, like so many of the Micronesians in this area of the Pacific, he crouched scowling in the rear of the boat with one hand on the motor control stalk whilst his eyes scanned the narrow channels surrounding us.

Infant rock islands grew out of the water like so many black mushrooms and in the darkness it was incredibly difficult to make out any route which would take us out to more open water.

Carefully and skillfully the boy threaded the boat between the miniature chunks of land, passing so close to some of them that I could have reached out to touch them.

Soon we were in a less congested area and we turned in a long sweeping curve around one of the larger islands until the bow was facing what I thought was due north.

Even further offshore the sea was still eerily calm and there was something rather sinister about being in an open boat off Palau's sombre coastline on such a night as this. As usual, the stars seemed much closer than they did on any of the main continents, the milky way stretching across the sky in one huge swathe of pale light almost from one horizon to the other.

I wondered what Lynne was thinking now she knew her husband was alive and had at last discovered where he was.

Her unwillingness to make the trip alone was understandable but she hadn't been as relieved as I'd expected her to be—or at least if she was she hadn't shown it. Until an hour ago I was sure she'd believed him to be dead yet, when she'd arrived at my door, I'd detected no real change in her manner and she hadn't seemed excited either at receiving his letter or at the prospect of meeting him.

Noel Webster had a lot of explaining to do. Not just to his wife but to me as well. For the first time I'd be able to talk to someone other than Inahara who knew about the diamonds and find out once and for all who it was that had been trying so hard to kill me. I might even get an explanation for the bullet holes in the Mercedes although I wasn't banking on that. I was, however, banking on the fact that Noel Webster would be waiting for Lynne by himself.

His note made it pretty clear he wanted to talk to her privately—presumably because he'd learned she'd arrived on Palau with friends and presumably because he wanted to justify his behaviour of the last few months to her before he did anything else. I imagined he'd persuade her to join forces with him. That would be very interesting—especially when Inahara found out.

Our voyage lasted rather longer than I'd anticipated, mainly because of our low speed but also as a result of our earlier excursions through the Rock Islands before we'd been able to turn north. It took nearly three quarters of an hour for us to approach the inlet where Webster was waiting for his wife.

Like a picture for a fairy story, Babelthuap was a vast black mountain of land rising out of the ocean. There was not a glimmer of light along any part of the low shoreline I could see and the smell of swamp and jungle was as strong as if we'd been in the centre of the island itself.

The noise of our motor would have alerted anyone waiting for us at the mouth of the Airai inlet long ago. I hoped it hadn't alerted anyone other than Lynne's husband. In a moment we were going to find out.

No more than a hundred yards from shore a narrow beam of light licked out over the water towards us. It wasn't a signal.

The beam travelled purposefully backwards and forwards along the boat whilst whoever was directing it counted the number of passengers on board. There was nothing I could do but sit where I was and hope he wouldn't try anything rash before we landed.

The boat grounded long before we reached the source of the light. Our engine stalled as our bow nudged into the soft bottom of the inlet and we were suddenly left in darkness again.

Jumping over the side, the islander made an attempt to shove us a few more feet but abandoned the job as hopeless.

I gave Lynne a hand then stepped out into ankle deep water covering two feet of mud having the consistency of thick porridge. The mud felt even warmer than the water.

The three of us slurped our way towards a low bank of reeds where we'd last seen the light.

I felt particularly vulnerable and spent a few anxious seconds wondering if I'd been foolish in arriving so openly to face what Inahara called the opposition.

Shortly before we reached the bank the light came on again, this time hitting me squarely in the eyes. I couldn't see a thing.

"Turn that bloody thing off," I shouted angrily.

"Noel," Lynne called out.

The beam switched briefly to her then swung downwards to illuminate a patch of harder mud where Webster was standing. At least I hoped it was Webster. He didn't answer his wife.

Before he could direct his flashlight at me again I transferred the Walther from my pocket to my belt then struggled the last few feet to more solid ground.

"Noel," Lynne queried again more quietly.

"Here."

She turned towards the voice.

"Over here, Lynne."

She went forward to stand in front of the figure of a man I could just make out as my eyes recovered from the effect of the light.

"I damn well told you to come alone." The voice was high and sounded strained.

"This is Daniel Chase," Lynne said. "Daniel, come here and meet my husband."

I approached Webster wondering if the occasion required me to shake hands. I thought his reception of Lynne hadn't been exactly warm.

"Lynne asked me to come with her," I explained. "I'm sure you understand."

I couldn't see him properly but I sensed tremendous hostility and fear.

"You're a fool," he hissed so quietly I could hardly hear him.

Lynne reached out to touch him but he swung on his heel and began walking away.

"Noel," she said. "Please."

"Follow me to the house. It isn't far." He spoke more normally but I was sure I could still detect an underlying fear.

"Lynne," I said. "We can't just walk into this. I know

he's your husband but don't forget what happened to our car back in Honolulu and remember someone tried to shoot us up when we were in Guam. We're not going to any house until we've had a talk first."

"I know," she whispered. "Something's awfully wrong. He isn't even pleased to see me."

"Webster," I shouted, "hang on a minute."

He came back. "What for?"

"Two things. First of all your wife's come half way across the world to find you and all you can say is 'I told you to come alone.' I think that's pretty lousy. Secondly, you and I have got some talking to do and if you think I'm following you into some kind of trap you've got rocks in your head."

Moving his face close to mine, he spat out his words. "You're a stupid fool, Chase — I'm disappointed. Now are you coming with me or not?"

Lynne made another attempt to touch his arm. "Noel, I know about the diamonds and everything but something's the matter — I know something else is wrong."

He shrugged her off.

I had made up my mind. "We're not going anywhere with you, Webster," I said with as much edge to my voice as I could muster.

He laughed. A hard, false laugh. "Suit yourself, dummy." Raising his flashlight he sent three quick bursts in the direction of the jungle.

The violence of the last few days had tempered me. I wasn't going to mess about.

I smashed the muzzle of the Walther straight across the side of his face, grabbed Lynne roughly by the arm and began to run.

Protesting, she started struggling as I dragged her back towards the boat.

I'd reacted just in time.

Powerful lights flickered out from at least three different places on the foot hills.

"For Christ's sake shut up," I yelled at her. "Just move."

Someone was shouting my name. It didn't sound like Webster's voice.

"Chase, stay where you are or you're a dead man."

Like searchlights, the beams were crisscrossing the mud flats all around us. Long before we reached the boat they were going to pick us up whilst we wallowed up to our knees in mud and water.

I changed direction, heading along the shore towards the nearest patch of dark jungle. It was hard going even though Lynne had stopped fighting me. Already it was difficult to find enough breath.

In front of us, the boy who had brought us here rose silently out of the reeds. He held a thick tree branch in one hand.

He was too slow by half. Before he was fully on his feet I kicked him savagely in the stomach, wrenched his weapon from his grasp and left him writhing in the mud.

For a fraction of a second one of the lights picked us up but it overshot to pause on a scrubby mangrove. Perhaps they hadn't seen us.

I bargained on the fact that Lynne had got the message by now.

"You go on," I said. "Get into the jungle over there and wait for me. Go!"

She didn't argue. Running swiftly between the reed banks she successfully eluded the beam and vanished into the night.

Whoever was directing the light must have had his suspicions.

As I began following Lynne he found me. This time he didn't overswing.

Unable to see anything but blinding white light I was forced to turn away from it in a vain attempt to escape.

Another light joined the first one and more men were shouting my name. I was scared to bloody death.

Vaulting over a rotten log I ran like hell to the nearest estuary, diving headlong over the bank as the first bullets zipped past to thud into the ground beside me.

Terrified, I crawled on hands and knees towards the water then turned to begin slithering my way across the mud in the shelter of a low bank which concealed me from the lights. It was a painfully slow business but it was safe.

For the next fifty yards I travelled on my stomach listening to more instructions for me to stop being stupid. If they really expected me to stand up it certainly wasn't me who was being stupid.

Another few yards and I'd be in the protection of the trees.

"Lynn," I called softly.

"Over here, Daniel."

Like some swamp animal, with mud in my eyes, ears and mouth, I fought my way through liquid muck until my hands gripped the first strands of reed grass.

Hauling myself onto a hard plateau formed by the roots of giant mangroves I peered back towards the main estuary.

They knew they'd lost us. Ranging from perhaps half a mile in each direction the beams lacked their earlier precision and were sweeping the mudflats and foreshore in an aimless pattern.

I used a handful of grass to wipe my face and hands. The noise of a breaking twig told me where Lynne was.

"Here," I whispered.

"Are you hurt? I heard the shooting." She appeared from nowhere to stand in front of me.

I stood up and spat out some more mud. "I'm okay. Sorry I shoved you around like that—there wasn't time to explain."

I didn't know what to say about her husband. There wasn't much I could say when I didn't even really know what had gone wrong. But I was sure of two things. We were in one hell of a fix and, for the next few hours, the pair of us had better concentrate on nothing but plain survival. Right now I couldn't bother about Noel Webster or the strange meeting with his wife I'd witnessed, there would be plenty of time to do that once we got out of here.

My Walther was heavily smeared in mud but I'd managed to keep it free from the more glutinous stuff. Although the action was certain to jam on the second round, in an emergency it'd probably fire the one already in the breech.

Astonishingly my flashlight had remained stuck firmly in my pocket. Not daring to try it for fear of attracting attention, I dismantled it, poured out the water and used Lynne's handkerchief to dry the batteries. When I'd finished I was ready to move on.

Knowing it was essential to stay close to the coast in a jungle covered island like Babelthuap, I'd already figured out the only plan which would give us a chance. Keep moving away from the Airai estuary until dawn when, with any luck at all, we'd be able to locate a village and decide how best to get back to Koror. I hoped we wouldn't have to fight our way there.

Taking Lynne's hand I began to lead her through the trees trying to establish a route which would take us midway between the softer mud and the much thicker vegetation further inland.

It was pretty tough, not just because it was so damned dark, but because of numerous fresh water lagoons which inevitably proved much deeper than I'd expected.

In case of pursuit I kept up a pace which I thought would guarantee our safety. Stumbling over exposed mangrove roots and gasping for breath, we paused in a particularly overgrown area of the swamp to get our bearings. Unless I was prepared to take a chance on getting lost I knew we'd have to change direction slightly and head more towards the shore. If we did that, progress would be easier as long as we didn't hit more mud.

To avoid wading waist deep through the nearest lagoon before striking off further to the south, I elected to skirt round it venturing into an extremely dense patch of trees.

Suddenly Lynne jerked my hand. "Listen!"

From our right something was approaching. And from two other directions similar noises told me we were no longer alone.

I felt prickling on the back of my neck. Gun ready I chanced a quick flash of light.

And there, mouth open, twenty feet away was one of Palau's other inhabitants.

A fully grown, very angry crocodile.

TEN

It was an impossible choice. If I used either flashlight or gun, Noel Webster's friends with their rifles and spot lamps would know exactly where to find us. But, without light and with no means of defence other than the Walther, we were at the mercy of God knows how many crocodiles which were living here in the swamp. The one I'd seen had been all of eight feet long and hadn't just looked angry, it'd been hell bent on attack and, although the light seemed to have stopped it temporarily, the damn thing could just be waiting for us to make a move.

I couldn't hear anything but the thudding of my heart.

Saturated in warm water and perspiration, until a moment ago I'd been unbearably hot. Now I felt a chill of fear start crawling all over me.

I remembered another night years ago deep beneath the Coral Sea when my lights had failed. That time it had been a single creature. A tiger shark unwilling to close in as long as I'd been able to poke a kilowatt beam at him. I still got nightmares about the long haul to the surface with half my shoulder ripped open and my air bubbling away as I fought to stay alive.

"Don't move," Lynne whispered. "Keep absolutely still."

Cursing my stupidity at not cleaning the Walther properly, I tried the action experimentally, feeling it jam on particles of gritty mud.

I strained my ears and eyes whilst trying to decide if I should risk using the flashlight again.

"They're fresh water crocodiles," Lynne said very quietly.

"I don't think they'll attack us in the dark. They're not large enough."

Judging by the size of his mouth and the mean look in his eyes, the one I'd shone the light at hadn't felt outclassed one little bit. I was sure I could smell its breath mixing with the damp, fetid odour from the swamp.

There was a loud splash right in front of us.

Flashlight in one hand and gun in the other, I tensed ready. Then, by deliberately looking slightly away from the place I'd heard the noise, I finally got my peripheral vision to work.

Still about twenty feet away, I saw the shape of it moving out of the lagoon onto the plateau. An efficient reptile hunting in an environment which was its home, there was nothing ungainly or lumbering about it. At the same time, from the other corner of my eye, I picked out another two, or at least I thought the dark humps I could discern were crocodiles.

"Can you see anything at all?" I whispered.

"No."

I reached out and placed my hand on the top of her head making her turn it slowly from side to side. "Don't look right ahead," I said. "Use the corners of your eyes."

"Got them," she said. "I think so, anyway. Two over there. They're not moving, Daniel."

"You watch those. I can see the other one."

For all I knew there could be dozens, but I was less rattled now we'd pin pointed three even though we couldn't see them well enough to know what they had in mind.

I snatched a glance at my watch. Nearly four o'clock. Dawn wasn't far away and, although the prospect was hardly inviting, if we had to, we could stand right here for the remainder of the night.

Making the same slithering noise I'd heard before, the crocodile I'd been watching was melting into the twisted shapes of the mangroves.

Straining to keep it in sight I willed my irises open but it was no use — I could almost imagine it had never been there at all.

"Can you see yours?" I whispered anxiously.

"Yes, but I'm not sure they're crocodiles any more, they still haven't moved."

I knew we couldn't continue like this. Being ripped to pieces in some God forsaken Pacific island swamp was no way to die and anyway I wasn't nearly ready to go, this way or any other.

Spending the next few hours in the middle of a crocodile filled swamp with my nerves stretched taut was going to be impossible. It wasn't a solution to our predicament and we'd still have to find our way out in the morning when the crocs could see us better. There had to be a better way.

"What are we going to do?" Lynne whispered.

If Lynne's husband had been living nearby, there was every probability he'd known the swamp was infested with these things and, if he had any sense, he'd leave us to live or die in here, depending on our talent for survival. Now I thought about it, one thing seemed certain — no-one was going to follow us. I also thought it was a hell of a way for Webster to treat his wife.

There was nothing for it but to adopt the philosophy which had worked on the few other occasions in my life when I'd been in a tight spot.

I pointed the flashlight at the animals Lynne was watching and pushed down firmly on the button.

She'd been right, they hadn't moved. Decaying logs tend to stay in the same place for days on end. I switched off the light, wondering if anyone had seen it and whether it really mattered or not.

"We're going to mortgage some of our luck and keep going," I said. "But we'll have to put up with the mud on the beach. Now we know what lives around here I don't think anyone's going to come looking for us until daylight.

So, Mrs Webster, we take our chance with these things until we get out of the mangroves."

"It's my fault again, isn't it? It's always my fault." She sounded close to panic.

"I wouldn't know. From what I've seen tonight I don't understand why the hell you wanted to find your husband to begin with. And, on top of that, I think you might have told me a pack of lies—but the inquest can wait. Come on, let's move."

I reckoned we were about a quarter of a mile inland, if inland was the right name for a jungle swamp. Before the crocodiles had stopped us in our tracks I'd intended striking off diagonally towards the sea—this time I made directly for the ocean by the fastest route. I was going to move swiftly, prepared to fight for every yard of the way.

It was a nerve racking business. Knowing that at any second a pair of gaping jaws could appear out of nowhere, splashing and stumbling we entered the dark lagoon ahead of us.

"If we can make enough noise we might frighten them off," Lynne gasped.

I was holding the flashlight and gun above my head to keep them dry and praying I wouldn't trip on the network of slimy roots lining the bottom of the lagoon. Even if I'd wanted to I couldn't have made any more noise than I was already.

Only yards away from solid ground, something warned me of impending disaster. Like a fool I stopped walking, cautioning Lynne to stand still for a moment whilst I tried to determine which of my senses had sounded the alarm.

When I spun round it was close enough for me to see its beady eyes glinting in the beam from the flashlight.

Slamming together like a pair of nail studded planks, its jaws enveloped Lynne's right arm from elbow to wrist and in less than a second she was fighting for her life.

Before I could move, she was pulled backwards into the

water, her screams turning into a dreadful bubbling noise as her head went under.

Frantically seizing a disappearing foot I tried clawing my way along her body towards the animal's head but the crocodile was already rolling, wrenching her away from me into deeper water.

For a second I lost her, then my fingers wound themselves in her hair and I was able to launch myself forwards with the Walther outstretched ready in my other hand. From a distance of two feet, I smashed the barrel into one of its eyes, but it was like hitting a rotten log and served only to enrage it.

Wildly thrashing its tail, it was deliberately keeping Lynne's head beneath the water and unless I could make the bastard let her go very quickly, I knew she was going to drown. Despairingly, I realised it was futile to even try stopping it from dragging us further away from shore.

One slender chance that I could save her — just one.

My fingers still tangled in her hair, I slipped underwater using her trapped arm to guide the Walther into the narrow gap between the animal's teeth.

God, there wasn't enough room. Using every ounce of my strength I rammed harder until suddenly my whole forearm slipped deep inside it's jaws.

I closed my eyes and jerked the trigger.

In a huge fountain of blood and water, the entire front end of the gun blew up taking half the animal's head with it.

Lungs bursting, I surfaced and hauled Lynne away from the still moving carcase of the crocodile. She floated free but made no attempt to help herself. Dear God, had I been too late?

Disengaging my hand from her hair I carried her to shore where I threw her down on the mud and instantly applied mouth to mouth resuscitation praying for some response. Four, five, six breaths — then on the seventh, as she exhaled under the action of my hands pushing on her chest, she coughed. I rolled her onto her side just before she vomited.

When she seemed capable of breathing unassisted, I left her for a second and began searching for my lost flashlight on the edge of the lagoon, hoping the commotion might have washed it into the shallows.

Unable to see more than a few inches through the filth that had been stirred up I abandoned the job and returned to where I'd left her. Still coughing, she was trying to sit up.

"Oh God, Daniel." She tilted forwards into my arms.

Swearing inwardly at the loss of the precious flashlight, as the full impact of what happened began to filter through my head, I explored the deep punctures in her arm with my fingertips.

Her skin felt sticky and my fingers tasted of blood when I put them to my lips.

Ripping off the sleeve from my shirt I knotted it round her arm, using a stick to tighten it into a tourniquet. Then, gritting my teeth, I picked her up and embarked upon one of the toughest jobs I'd had to face for a very long time.

Staggering under her weight, my feet banging into every single stump lying between the lagoon and the sea, I lurched off into the darkness bound for the only place where we might be safe for what remained of the night.

John was carrying two very tall glasses filled with ice, a delicious looking pale yellow liquid and bits of lemon.

"I'm told this'll fix anything," he said handing me one. "Vodka and crocodile blood."

I sat up in bed and took it from him. "How long have I been asleep?"

"It's four o'clock. You crashed about ten this morning so you've only wasted most of the day."

"How's Lynne?"

"Don't know exactly but she's bound to be okay. Inahara fixed up the holes in her arm, gave her a shot and we put her to bed just after you said you thought you'd get your head down for an hour."

The drink was even better than I'd expected. I reached for my cigarettes, lit one and drew in a lung full of smoke.

John shook his head. "You do a big rescue job on Lynne Webster, blow up a crocodile, steal a boat and then you sit there and fill yourself up with so much smoke you'll be lucky if you reach fifty."

I grinned at him. "I know I'm stupid. Inahara didn't stop telling me until I went to bed."

"I'm with him. I can't figure out why you offered to go with her, either—you must've known you were walking into trouble. Come on, Daniel old buddy, tell me why you really went?" He leaned forward.

I still had no intention of mentioning the bullet holes in the Mercedes but I knew I'd have to offer some sort of explanation if I wanted to avoid appearing unnecessarily foolish.

"I thought I might be able to do a deal with Noel Webster," I lied.

"But you found out he was scared out of his mind so you didn't bother?"

"Right," I said. "It wasn't much of an idea, anyway."

He narrowed his eyes. "I don't believe you. You didn't go to do a deal—I know damn well you wouldn't try a double cross. If I thought you were that kind of guy I wouldn't have come this far with you."

"Okay, okay. So that wasn't why I went. I'm not going to tell you my reason—will you buy that?"

"Yeah. I guess you know what you're doing."

"I'm not sure yet—I'll let you know when I'm further along with some other ideas I've got." I wished it was true.

He sat down on the end of the bed and drained his glass.

"You're a funny bastard."

"Thanks."

He lowered his eyes for a moment. "First you save my life, now you've just saved Lynne's, but you don't give a damn, do you? Lynne kept on saying her husband tried to kill you. Do you have any ideas about that?"

"No, just a feeling he's being used or doesn't know what's going on. I'm not too sure he tried to shoot me, anyway. He didn't have a gun when I saw him."

"Inahara wants us to go out to the site tomorrow, did he tell you?"

I nodded. "I'll be okay. The sooner we find that aircraft the sooner we might get some answers."

John stood up. "That Inahara's a clever guy, do you know that? He put three stitches in Lynne's arm, cleaned out every damn hole from the croc's teeth like he was a doctor and used a hypodermic as though he'd been doing it all his life."

"Maybe he's too clever for both of us."

"Yeah, maybe. We'll see. I've got to go and take your boat back now. Inahara's going to follow in a launch we hired this afternoon. I really came to ask you where you borrowed it from." He unfolded a map of Babelthuap on the bed. "Give me a rough idea."

The Airai inlet was shown as a nice clean mud free slot in the coast. Whoever had drawn the map either had a warped sense of humour or had never bothered to visit the place at low tide.

I put my finger on the spot where I thought we'd landed. "That's where we met Webster."

Tracing our progress along the green coloured coastline, I guessed at the point where we'd first run into the crocodiles then tried to estimate how far I'd travelled carrying Lynne. My memory of the last few miles wasn't too clear.

I'd encountered no more lagoons and seen no more

crocodiles on my way to the beach but, towards the end, with Lynne heavy in my arms and my exhaustion increasing with each footstep, the journey had rapidly turned into a test of physical endurance.

When I'd finally cleared the swamp country the mud hadn't been too bad but I could still recall the tremendous relief I'd experienced a quarter of an hour later at the feeling of real sand under my feet.

Dawn had been breaking when I'd thankfully lowered Lynne onto the beach where I'd washed her wounds in clear salt water. She'd lost some blood but the punctures had nearly closed up with the swelling and after a short rest she'd been capable of walking by herself until we'd come across a glass fibre boat I'd borrowed to bring us back here to Koror.

"Right there." I pointed to a tiny curved bay a couple of miles west of Airai. "The boat was moored to a red buoy about fifty yards off shore."

John refolded the map. "Okay. We'll be back for dinner. Inahara said for you to wake Lynne around five thirty. If she needs anything her favourite doctor'll be in attendance about six."

He collected my empty glass, winked and left the room.

The longer I knew John Hyland the more I liked him. Until last night the same had been true about the way I'd been drawn towards Lynne, but since meeting her husband I was no longer certain she'd told me the truth about him or about herself and I didn't know how I felt anymore.

I stubbed out my cigarette, climbed out of bed and wandered over to the shower. It was difficult if not impossible to decide whether Lynne was what she seemed, I wasn't a hundred percent sure about John yet and I'd given up trying to analyse Inahara days ago.

The hot water was pleasant on my skin. Increasing the pressure, I let the stinging jets hit me full in the face imagining them scouring away the last vestiges of Babel-thuap's stinking mud.

I stayed in the shower a long time, thinking round in circles for the hundredth time since I'd started out on this adventure back in Hawaii.

I emerged dripping wet still thinking.

Tying a towel round my waist I went back to the bedroom for another cigarette.

Someone was sitting in the swivel chair near the window.

I was beginning to get used to games like this.

Closing my fingers round the neck of a vase I crept forward ready to spring.

Before I reached my visitor he swung round in the chair and stared at me with very clear blue eyes.

He was a well built white man in his early thirties with thinning hair. Unshaven and dirty, his left cheek had been split open recently and his face was disfigured by an ugly bruise.

"Mr Chase," he said. "We meet again."

I recognised the voice. It was Noel Webster, the man I'd seen only in the dark on Babelthuap last night.

"Webster?"

He switched his eyes to the vase I was carrying then fingered his injured cheek. "I already owe you for this one. Don't push your luck, Chase."

I threw it on the bed. "I don't believe you're stupid enough to have come here just for that, but, in case you have, I'll tell you right now. Make one move to get out of that chair and I'll make sure you're carried out of here on a stretcher." I pointed a finger at him. "Your friends bloody near killed me last night and then you left your wife to die in the swamp. I've met some bastards, Webster, but you're top of my list. It'd be a real pleasure to take you apart."

"Have you finished?" There was no resentment in his voice and no suggestion of the fear I'd sensed last night.

"What do you want?"

"How about a cigarette for a start?"

When I'd lit one for myself I tossed him the packet and some matches. Then I sat on the bed waiting for him to explain what he was doing here.

"I came to see Lynne."

"Tough luck. She's under sedation with an armful of holes made by a crocodile we met last night after we'd said goodnight to you."

A trace of something flickered across his face. I didn't think it was pity.

"I told you last night you were a fool," he said shortly.

"I remember, but I don't much care what you think."

"That note I sent to Lynne. It was supposed to be a trap for you or Hyland. They made me do it."

"Who are they?"

"Never mind. They said they'd kill her—just her—unless I sent the note. They made me put in the bit about her coming alone to make damned sure you or Hyland would go with her to hold her hand. It worked nicely, didn't it?" He made an attempt to smile. "They were sure she wouldn't make the trip by herself—not even to see her long lost husband."

I took a long thoughtful drag on my cigarette. "Let me guess, Webster. They, whoever they are, made a deal with you. Lynne would be allowed to join you and stay alive so long as you laid the trap to get John Hyland or I onto Babelthuap. Right?"

He nodded. "You know where the aircraft is, don't you. We wanted to get the information out of you before you started diving."

"Don't tell me you've come to do a deal with me?"

"No, We'll wait now. When you got away last night they knew they'd blown it and tried to kill you. Without a diver Inahara would've been held up for a while and we could have had time to screw the information out of

Hyland. But, like I said, we'll let you take us to it now."

"So, what the hell do you want?"

"I came to see my wife, Chase. I wanted to explain."

"Explain to me. I'll tell her if I think it's a good idea."

He put his head in his hands. "You'd never understand."

"Try me."

He raised his head. "Lynne and I haven't had anything that's been any good for quite a while. It's a long story but I wanted to get some money—big money. My wife is a rich women, Chase, and I've never had any. It's always been between us even though she's always said it didn't matter to her. Sometimes I believed her but, even if it was true, it didn't help the way I felt.

Anyway, more by accident than anything else, I heard about this deal out here on Palau and decided this was my big chance—maybe the only one I'd ever get. Excitement and real money—I suppose it sounded good in London at the time. They didn't tell me the truth of course—just like you."

"What the hell do you mean?" The comment had been made idly but it sounded a warning bell in my brain.

"Forget it. You want the explanation so just listen. Once I'd arrived here and found out what was really going on it was too late to change my mind and, anyhow, I'd already been paid ten thousand and I'd got used to the idea of having more money than I'd ever dreamed of. I've just kept on from there, really.

Everything would still be alright if Lynne hadn't come looking for me. She's always been like that, Chase. Even though I know she doesn't love me, to her I'm still her husband and she's the kind of person who believes it's important to stay with it no matter how lousy a marriage turns out to be."

"What's your part of the deal?" I interrupted.

"I've done a bit of underwater work in my job, I'm a marine biologist. I was supposed to get my share for cutting the stuff out of the submarine — nice easy money. If the bloody plane hadn't gone down it'd all be over now and I'd have all the money. And Lynne wouldn't have left England. We could have started over again." He looked at the floor. "I can't let her believe I hoped she'd die in the swamp, Chase. Sure, maybe I'm a bastard, but I knew about the crocodiles and if I hadn't been stopped I'd have got her out of there. You too."

"So you could persuade me to tell you where the Piper is. Thanks."

He shook his head. "I know how it sounds. You'd already be dead if it wasn't for me, though."

For the second time, something he'd said touched a nerve. "How's that? I don't remember hearing you telling your mates to stop trying to gun me down last night."

"Not last night. On Guam. I found out Lynne was travelling with you from the airport but they didn't know she was my wife then. I organised that roadblock, Chase. I had six Palau Islanders with me, four of them with rifles. It cost me five hundred US dollars to make sure they didn't hit the car. You don't know how lucky you were."

Everything slipped neatly into place. At last I understood. "And later you went to our hotel in Agana to punch those holes in the Mercedes?"

He was momentarily surprised at what I'd said. "I didn't think you knew about that. You see, I had to make it look good. Not just for you — for my friends, as you call them. If they'd known what I'd done I'd be dead by now. As it is, if they find out I've been here this afternoon I'll never get away from Palau alive. With Lynne here with you, they don't trust me any more."

"So you did it to save your wife. What about Inahara, Hyland and me?"

He shrugged. "You won't believe me, but I'm no killer, Chase. I don't know what I'd have done if Lynne hadn't have been with you. Who cares now?"

Discovering the truth behind the bullet holes in the Mercedes was an unexpected piece of luck and, but for some other doubts raised by what Webster had said, I felt a good deal happier than I'd been since we'd left Honolulu. At least I didn't have to worry about John and Inahara from now on.

I offered him another cigarette. I almost felt sorry for him. He refused. "Can I see Lynne?"

"I told you, she's out cold."

"Will you tell her for me, Chase?"

"Sure, but why not change sides or forget all about it? From what you've said, you've got nothing to lose."

"What about the rest of the money?"

"Christ, Webster, what about it? What about your marriage? What about your wife? She doesn't give a damn about the bloody money. Think, man, think!"

He peered at me vacantly for a moment. "It's too late. We'll win, anyway. You don't know what you're up against. I've got to go back now. Just do me a favour, Chase—in return for that ambush on Guam. Get Lynne on a plane back to England. It might save her life."

If I let him walk out on me I might never get answers to the questions swirling around inside my head. And I had to have the answers.

I stood up and walked over to his chair. "Maybe you can do me a favour."

"What?"

"Tell me exactly what I'm up against. Who are the people you're working for and why the hell are you so sure you're going to win?"

"I didn't come here to answer your questions."

"How do you fancy me smashing your head against the wall? If I believe what you've said what have I got to lose? I can make a real mess of you in five minutes."

He shook his head. "You're way out of your depth, Chase. Like I said, you're stupid."

Genuine anger welled up in my throat.

Grabbing him by the shirt front I hauled him roughly up out of the chair. "Now you listen to me you smart bastard, we'll start with a nice easy one. What the hell did you mean when you said I hadn't been told the truth?"

He laughed bitterly. "Last night on Babelthuap. Lynne said she knew about the diamonds and everything. You don't have to play at being a tough guy, Chase, you're welcome to the benefit of my experience. They told me it was gold bullion." He laughed again, a dreadful hollow laugh. "Gold bullion — diamonds — what a bloody joke."

I shook him fiercely. "What do you mean, Webster?"

Behind me, the door burst open, slamming back against the wall with such force that the top hinge tore right out of the woodwork.

Two Europeans stood in the corridor. Both held silenced automatics.

I began hauling Webster around in front of me but I'd hardly moved before they fired.

The first shot pierced his heart, the second left a neat and blood rimmed hole in the centre of his forehead.

Still dressed in nothing but my towel, I let his lifeless body slip from my grasp then turned to face the men who'd killed him.

Unable to either speak or move, my eyes drawn inexorably to the two guns pointing at my stomach, I waited for the end.

One of the men spoke to me. "Not this time, Chase. Right now you're the golden goose. But, if you don't remember who that stuff in the plane belongs to, we'll be back to say goodbye."

A warm pool of blood from Webster's body was already forming round my feet. Sickened by what had taken place in the last few seconds yet so unbelievably grateful that I was to be spared, I remained rooted to the floor.

Gradually recovering from the shock of being confronted with instant death from two armed strangers, I watched them lower their weapons and leave the doorway almost as suddenly as they had appeared.

ELEVEN

Wednesday morning, October 27th, an unspoilt Pacific morning so clear and bright it was hard to believe that nothing but death and violence had attended our mission since arriving on Palau. It was still cool and not a ripple marked the sea inside the reef for it was too early for the breeze to have realised dawn had broken over the Rock Islands.

In an hour's time, even well away from land on board our launch the Nova, I knew it would become uncomfortably hot and the sunshine would have a harsher quality about it. But, for a while, Palau's Rock Islands would retain their almost magic quality and each scrap of land would continue to cast its shadow on the water.

John was shouting at me.

I looked up at him from the deck of the launch. "What?"

"Lynne's coming down. Stop watching seagulls and give her a hand."

On the rickety jetty twelve feet above me John helped her onto the ladder, grasping her uninjured left arm as she placed her feet hesitantly on each of the wooden rungs.

When she was close enough I reached up and put my hands round her waist. "Okay, I've got you." She released John's hand and allowed me to lift her down.

"Thanks." She tried hard to smile but refused to meet my eyes. Turning her back on me she went into the cabin to join Inahara.

Carrying the last remaining items of our equipment,

John clambered down after her, jumping the last few feet onto the deck.

"She's a pretty cool one, isn't she?" he said.

"The way she took the news you mean?"

"Yeah. Seeing as how she's only been a widow since last night, she's come round real quick, don't you think?"

I shrugged. "Webster said their marriage hadn't been working. I'm sure she only came out here because she thought she had to—sort of a duty. After what happened on Babelthuap she must've known things were washed up for good."

John stowed one of the boxes on deck, lashing it down with a length of polypropylene rope. "Inahara said she didn't fold up when he told her last night. He didn't mention how or where it happened, of course. As far as she knows we just heard her husband was dead. This time she really believes it, though."

I changed the subject. "I found out something interesting before Webster died. I didn't mention it last night but you and I better have a talk as soon as we're underway."

There was a roar as Inahara started the big diesels.

"Mr Chase," he called out from the cabin. "Will you be kind enough to ask Mr Hyland to join us on board, I would like to leave immediately."

"He's already here," I shouted. "Are we ready to cast off?"

"Ah yes, Mr Chase. It would be good to be at sea on such a splendid morning, do you not think so?"

"It'll be even better underwater. How about coming down with me?"

His face appeared at the hatch. "It may prove essential for us to spend today laying a trail, Mr Chase. If, however, that is unnecessary you may persuade me to accompany you. Now let us explore these Rock Islands of which I have heard so much."

Leaving John to attend to the bow, I released the stern

warp and gave Inahara a thumbs up sign. He ducked back into the wheel house and eased open the throttles.

I hadn't discovered where Inahara had managed to hire the launch from. Knowing he'd only refer to the need for him to organise the project in the most efficient way possible, I'd stopped asking him questions about such things.

Forty feet long and fitted with powerful twin diesel engines, the launch was no more than five years old and obviously of American origin. Although extensively fitted out with big game fishing gear, it would serve admirably as a diving boat and, in the circumstances, Inahara couldn't really have made a better choice. It was far superior to a lot of boats I'd used for recovery jobs in the past, being completely self contained with plenty of room for the four of us and all my diving equipment. I thought I couldn't have wished for anything more.

With a satisfying burble from the exhausts we drew slowly away from Koror heading for the inevitable gap between the two nearest symmetrical green islands.

Free of the horizon now, the sun was a shimmering white disc, turning the smooth ocean from silvery grey to a pale azure colour. Dawn and sunrise over Palau was an event of exceptional beauty and it wasn't long before I began remembering some of the other times I'd been similarly moved by the birth of a Pacific morning on some lonely atoll or island where Jean, Gerry and I had based our camp before a dive. I was getting tired of memories but at least they seemed to be occurring less frequently of late.

On this occasion I had no brother-in-law and no wife to share the experience. Instead I had a friend, John Hyland; an unfathomable Japanese colleague who had told me we were diving for diamonds which I was almost certain we were not; and Lynne Webster, a strangely attractive girl and a woman whose husband's cruel murder I had witnessed in my own bedroom just over twelve hours ago.

John had been right when he'd said the trip might turn out to be interesting.

Compared to other trips I'd made there was another difference, too. Somewhere, out here among Palau's innocent baby islands, another group of men were waiting for us to show them where the Piper Aztec had died and come to rest on the ocean floor. I wasn't sure what might happen when they found out but Inahara was bound to have some idea how to handle the situation. That was his department and he could worry about it.

John had told me that Inahara had already mapped out an approximate route which would take us to the spot where the plane should be and I knew we'd have to navigate only a short passage through the islands before entering clearer water outside the reef.

There was something I had to do.

Entering the cabin I placed a hand gently on Lynne's shoulder "I know I said it last night but I need to say it once more. I'm sorry about your husband, Lynne. I didn't know him but he must have been a nice person to have made you want to come out here to find him. I'm just sorry we didn't find him in time. I mean that."

She turned to look at me. "It doesn't matter, anymore. I just want this finished with so I can go home." Her eyes were steady but her face was expressionless.

"You know you can't go home until it's over, don't you?"

"Yes, I know it's dangerous. Inahara's told me, John's told me and you've told me." She smiled faintly. "I do understand, you know."

I'd run out of words. There was nothing more to say. Leaving her, I went to find John. He was sitting cross legged on a hatch cover at the front of the cabin roof.

"Did you talk to her?" he asked.

"Yes. She's alright."

"You'd be glad about that, Daniel, wouldn't you?"

"Hell, I don't know. Before I met her husband I thought

I had her figured out — and myself figured out, too. Now I don't know. None of your business, anyway."

He appeared hurt. An uncharacteristic reaction for John Hyland.

"It's okay," I grinned at him. "I didn't mean it that way. We'll see what happens. I've got too many hang ups to bother about it now, or any other time, probably."

"What did you want to talk to me about?"

"Two things. About diamonds, but that'll wait. I'd better get something else off my chest first."

Starting with my discovery of the bullet holes in the Mercedes, I told him about my earlier suspicions, explaining how I'd begun to distrust both him and Inahara and how I'd gone to Babelthuap hoping to find an answer.

After I told him how Webster had arranged the whole thing and answered his questions, I outlined what else I'd learned from Lynne's husband minutes before his death.

He didn't look particularly surprised. "So it wasn't diamonds after all," he said calmly.

"Doesn't sound like it. And Webster made it fairly clear it wasn't gold, either."

He put his hands behind his head and stretched. "Then what about Inahara's submarine? I thought the story sounded pretty good. I believed it."

I nodded. "I think I still believe it. What we've got to do is substitute something for diamonds — something the Japanese Government wants to get it's hands on in a hurry."

"And something these other guys want real badly, too." John screwed up his face whilst he thought. "Maybe we should stop worrying about it. You're going to find out soon. At least, if I've done my calculations right, you will."

"I still want to know what we're really looking for," I said.

"Ask Inahara."

"Perhaps I will."

He clambered to his feet. "I'm glad I came, Daniel old buddy. So far it's turned out a whole lot better than I thought it'd be." He swept his hand across the tremendous vista of the Rock Islands on our starboard bow. "That's all ours for as long as we damn well want. I like being here, do you know that?"

"Someone's hanging around out there in those islands," I reminded him. "How do you feel about sharing Palau with Webster's friends?"

"Haven't met them yet but from what you've said, I reckon they might all go the same way as Webster did — you know fight amongst themselves. Either that or Inahara'll fix them. So long as we keep on working together and so long as luck holds out we'll come out of this on the top of the pile — you see."

"What did you do with Webster's body?" I asked.

"Took it out in the boat last night, tied half a dozen rocks to him and dropped him over the side. Hope we haven't given the local sharks the flavour."

"I'm not worried about sharks. I'm worried about Webster's friends — or who he thought were his friends, poor bastard. Like you said, you haven't met them — I've seen them in action."

"Let's go and talk to Inahara and see what he's got in mind."

I stood up. "Bet you a hundred dollars he's got it all sorted out."

John grinned. "You go easy. We haven't been paid yet."

Koror lay two or three miles in the distance now, a dark green mound at the foot of Babelthuap towering protectively behind the smaller island as if standing guard over Palau's offspring. There wasn't another vessel in sight and it was impossible to detect any sign of activity on any of the islands which I could see.

Inahara had spread out John's map on the chart table in front of him and was dividing his time between a study of the binnacle compass and the map coordinates which John had drawn for him.

Alongside the map, still wrapped in waxed paper, two brand new hand bearing compasses lay in their boxes ready for use.

John and Inahara had already decided how we were going to pin point the spot where I was going to make my first exploratory dive. Using both compasses simultaneously in a straightforward triangulation technique, we would rely on two landmarks back on Koror to align ourselves with the coordinates we'd calculated. How close we'd get remained to be seen but John seemed confident the system would work.

"Do you reckon we're being watched?" I asked Inahara.

"Although I cannot be sure, I believe that must be true, Mr Chase."

"Then we don't really want to hang about, do we? How about the dive?"

"I mentioned a false trail before. I hope we will be able to use the compasses to good advantage whilst we are moving—providing we reduce speed, of course. When we appear to be in the correct position, Mrs Webster will drop this over the side." He handed me a conically ended steel cylinder about four inches in diameter and nearly a foot long.

"What is it?" John enquired.

"A radio transmitter," I said. "Is that right, Inahara?"

"Indeed. It will allow us to return to the correct position during the hours of darkness, if it proves necessary. Perhaps Mr Chase will be fortunate enough to locate the aircraft using underwater lights."

"I didn't bother to announce my doubts. Night diving is not the best way to find things on the bottom of the sea and I hoped it wouldn't come to that. Not long from now I was going to discover how wrong I'd been.

Inahara continued speaking. "Once we have marked the

place where we believe the Piper to be, it is my intention to continue our voyage and pretend we are searching elsewhere. It will not be long before we will be too far from the islands for anyone to know what we are doing unless they follow us by boat and, if we are being watched, I anticipate that we will soon be joined at sea. Now, if you and Mr Hyland will take your compasses and prepare to sight onto your landmarks I will endeavour to steer to your instructions."

Before we began I had one last question. "Inahara, you know these people might try and board us, don't you?"

He turned and grinned at me. "We have three rifles and a sub machine gun to dissuade them should they attempt anything so foolish, Mr Chase."

I gave John one of the compasses, took the other myself and climbed up onto the cabin top.

Flicking up the sights I squinted over the dial at my landmark, a deep ravine cutting through the coastline some miles behind us.

"Can you see the hill?" I asked John.

"Can't miss the bloody thing. I hope it's going to be accurate enough. Maybe I should've chosen something smaller."

I started calling out instructions to Inahara, requesting a heading which would allow the ravine to align with the compass reading John had given me. At the same time, alternating with my directions, John began shouting out his own instructions.

Although Inahara had by far the hardest job in trying to strike a course which eventually would satisfy both John and me, to some extent, all three of us acted like a single, if rather inefficient, computer.

Our technique improved with practice and, as we gradually approached the point where our courses would cross, I could feel my excitement growing. Twenty minutes later we were close.

The launch barely moving now, Lynne hung over the bow ready to drop the transmitter.

"Okay," I said. "Keep it there, Inahara, that's good."

"Any second," John shouted. "Hold it. Okay, okay—let it go."

There was a splash as the transmitter disappeared and the job was done. After hours of work, days of expectation, and everything else which had happened, the event was a huge anti-climax.

Leaving John and me to continue peering over our compasses as though we were still intent on charting our route, Inahara imperceptably changed course, heading further south as he increased our speed again. I wondered if anyone was watching us after all.

Lynne passed me some binoculars. "Inahara said see if you can find out where their boat is."

"Don't bother," John answered. "Look." He pointed due west towards one of the larger channels in the chain of islands.

Two miles away another launch was heading out to sea leaving a long white wake behind it.

The binoculars were not much help, but I could see enough to establish that it was no accident the skipper of the vessel had struck a course which would guarantee interception if we maintained our present heading.

"And what are you able to see, Mr Chase?" Inahara had left the wheel-house.

"Nothing, but we can all guess who it is, can't we?"

"I believe so. We will prepare ourselves for company. It will be interesting to meet our opponents at last, I think."

Ten minutes later our opponents, as Inahara had called them, were close enough for us to count their numbers.

Bigger than the Nova and trailing a small dinghy, their boat was travelling very fast, the noise from its engines booming across the water ahead of it.

Inahara throttled back our own diesels, leaving them idling whilst we waited.

Still lying the cabin top, John and I exchanged binoculars and compass for a high powered 7.25mm rifle each. Inahara stood in the door of the wheel-house with his submachine gun cradled in his arms. He looked as solid as an old tree stump and his white teeth were gleaming in a characteristic grin of anticipation. A tough one, I thought —I hadn't ever met anyone quite like Inahara.

I wasn't sure whether I was nervous or not. It didn't seem likely that the encounter would turn into a fight but recent experience told me I should expect the unexpected.

"Mrs Webster, please be ready to pull back on the throttle levers the moment I ask you." Inahara joined us on the cabin top.

"Seven of them." John said quietly.

"Two each and one for Mrs Webster," Inahara replied equally quietly. "Let us show them we are not asleep."

He borrowed my rifle, steadied himself and drilled a neat hole clean through the bow of the approaching craft.

His action had been smooth, efficient and, despite the fact that the Nova wasn't moving, the shot had been remarkable. It also clearly demonstrated that we were not to be crowded.

The other boat slowed by reversing her props then dropped her anchor. She had OUVEA NEW CALEDONIA written on her stern.

Two men climbed into the dinghy and began rowing over to us.

I thought they must be pretty sure of themselves.

"Ah," Inahara said, inspecting our visitors with the binoculars. "It is as I thought." He left us and went to the rail. I noted that he hadn't left his gun behind and his face had hardened.

The two men who boarded the Nova were the men who had killed Noel Webster in my room. I recognised them with a mixture of slight apprehension and raw hostility. One of them nodded at me.

They spoke quietly to Inahara for several minutes whilst standing in the cockpit.

"Friends of yours?" John asked in a low voice.

"Widow makers," I whispered so Lynne couldn't over-hear. "I think Inahara knows them. I wonder what the hell's going on?"

I heard Inahara tell them to wait then he turned and waved us down to join him.

Dressed in filthy jeans and what had once been white shirts, both men were scruffy, dirty and over confident. Although Webster had been a weak man, he hadn't deserved to die at the hands of his own kind and for a second I could have turned my rifle on them and killed them as coldly as they'd killed him.

"Gentlemen," Inahara said to us. "Allow me to introduce Mr Julian French and Mr Peter Bishop. Do not, however, bother to shake hands with them, they are leaving im-mediately."

French was the one who had spoken to me in the hotel. Running to fat with thick lips and extremely small eyes, he was standing with his hands in his pockets inspecting Lynne through the cabin door.

Bishop was less of a slob to look at but appeared somewhat ill at ease. He had the kind of face which you find around the islands. The face of a thoroughly dissipated European who had lived the wrong kind of life. I couldn't stop remembering how they'd shot Webster.

"They have come to make us an offer," Inahara explained. He turned to French. "If I understand you correctly, you are prepared to share equally in what you regard as spoils from the sunken submarine. You suggest, in fact, that we work together and that we trust you."

"You think you're one hell of a smart Jap, don't you?" French couldn't know the manner of man he was addressing. I thought he was particularly stupid to under-rate Inahara so quickly. No-one in their right mind would treat him lightly — not the way he looked right now.

"Not at all, Mr French. I just wish to make it plain that my friends and I are not interested in your proposition. Please return to your boat at once and inform whoever you are working for that it would be inadvisable for him to continue meddling in my affairs."

For an answer, Bishop climbed onto the cockpit coaming and waved both hands at the men on the other boat. "Take a look, Jap," he said.

Fifty yards away, three men were stripping back a tarpaulin from something on the foredeck. When they'd finished, the twin barrels of a World War II anti-aircraft gun were pointing directly at the Nova. From its outline, the most deadly of its generation — a genuine Oerlikon. A gun with sufficient fire power to rip us to pieces in one burst.

"Beauty, isn't it?" Bishop remarked. "Surprising what you can pick up in the Philippines if you look around. You want a fight — that's fine. Save Mrs Webster for us, though — it'd be a shame to spoil her."

I could sense John's temper rising as he stood beside me. Handing me his rifle he stepped forwards but Inahara reached out an arm to stop him.

"Mr Hyland, do not bother yourself. These men are but pawns. Island trash who live like rats on the garbage and misery of others. They have been sent here by another man who would perhaps be more worthy of your attention."

I saw French's face twist. "Inahara, we'll blow this boat clear out of the water, leave you for the sharks and take the girl back to play with while we do our own diving. We can find that aircraft easy enough and we don't need no smart arsed aeronautical expert or no worn out diver to help us, either."

"Then your visit has certainly been unnecessary," Inahara

smiled coldly. He turned to me. "Mr Chase, please prepare
to kill anyone approaching the anti-aircraft gun. Mr
Hyland, perhaps you would take over the controls from
Mrs Webster whilst I escort these gentlemen off our boat."

"Don't try anything smart, Inahara," French warned.
"We came to make a deal, that's all." His tone had
changed.

"At once, Mr Hyland, full throttle if you will."

Climbing back onto the wheel-house I lay down and
centred my sights on the Oerlikon wondering what was
going to happen next.

Several things happened at once.

The instant John gunned our engines, men began
scrambling towards the Oerlikon. The bow of our launch
rose out of the water as we began to accelerate and trying
to line up my rifle on the Ouvea became a sheer
impossibility.

I squeezed off a dozen rounds in more or less the right
direction, nearly rolled off the cabin top as John put the
Nova into a turn and then looked round to see what
Inahara was doing.

Half in fascination, half in horror I saw he had gripped
Bishop and French by their throats and single handed was
in the process of strangling them to death.

Both men were raining blow after blow upon his head
and shoulders but his huge hands continued to bite into
their necks and he seemed oblivious to their inneffectual
yet desperate attempts to free themselves.

"Inahara," I shouted.

Like a bloody executioner he stood there, his eyes
without mercy and his hands squeezing the life out of
them. His face was nothing but a mask.

Now there was a deep roar from the engines as our
propellers cut powerfully into the water and spray was
gushing over the bow each time John spun the wheel. We
were really moving.

Scrambling down into the cockpit, I grabbed one of Inahara's arms and yelled in his ear. "Inahara!"

His face contorted, then, as though they were no more than plastic dolls, in one tremendous heave he lifted his victims clear of the deck and hurled them bodily over the stern into the wake.

"Cut the rope of the dinghy, Mr Chase." He flexed his fingers and looked upwards to the sky. "They are not dead, Daniel, but perhaps there will be another time when I cannot be persuaded to allow such men to live. You do not yet understand, but you were right to stop me."

He'd never called me Daniel before and, although they deserved to die, I certainly didn't understand. But, as I heard the first awful stutter from the Oerlikon and the shriek of shells filled my ears, I knew it didn't matter.

Hopelessly outgunned and with only John's skill at the wheel to save us, I was about to discover if anything was ever going to matter again.

TWELVE

Firing from the still stationary Ouvea, they couldn't miss us.

A third of the way back from the bow, the first earsplitting salvo tore an enormous hole through both sides of our hull as though it was made of paper. Long slivers of wood were driven back into the cabin with such violence that two of them buried themselves almost completely in the leather covered seats. And above the noise of it all, John was yelling for us to hold on.

For a fraction of a second the Nova shuddered then, as John spun the wheel again, she seemed to leap away from the other boat.

None of us had been injured by the flying splinters, the hole in our hull was several feet above the waterline and by the time the Oerlikon fired again we were moving in a series of wild curves on our way back to the Rock Islands. I unclenched my teeth, breathed again and thought that truly the gods had been kind to us.

More shells hissed viciously across our stern, the noise of them turning my blood to water. I grabbed my rifle, knelt down on the cockpit floor and tried desperately to keep my sights on the Ouvea whilst I fired round after round at her across the water. Just one lucky shot might make the difference. The distance between us was increasing by the second but once the gunner had our range, 20mm shells from the Oerlikon would shred us into so much matchwood if John couldn't keep us out of trouble.

They'd dragged French and Bishop out of the water now

and over my rifle barrel I saw the wave start to curl up over the bow of the Ouvea as she began the chase in earnest.

Using John's rifle to double our fire power, Inahara knelt beside me, but against an anti-aircraft gun our defence was pathetic. For the first time since I'd met him he didn't look confident. The biggest optimist in the world wouldn't have given two cents for our chances.

"Lynne," I yelled. "Chuck out some more ammunition. Quickly!"

I reloaded, frantically changing sides of the boat whilst John put the Nova into a turn so tight it was a miracle we didn't flip over.

Gallons of water poured into the cockpit through our shattered hull as more shells screamed into our wake. They threw up a line of miniature water spouts which approached us at alarming speed.

Whether it was John's fearful turn that saved us or whether the gunner couldn't see where his shells were landing I shall never know. Whatever the reason, for the third time we escaped total destruction by a scant few feet.

Now things were more difficult for those on board the Ouvea. She was moving very fast and, although she wasn't attempting to copy John's violent manoeuvres, her gunner's job would be much harder than before.

The stench of burning oil from our overworked diesels filled the cabin, and the cockpit decking was awash with water, debris from the cabin and used cartridge cases.

Literally throwing ourselves from one gunwhale to the other, Inahara and I were firing continuously using handfuls of spare ammunition clips which Lynne tossed out to us with her one good arm. The barrel of my rifle grew hot to touch.

Taking a less tortuous path through the water, the Ouvea was steadily gaining on us. A thousand yards behind she fired one long terrifying burst.

Ten feet ahead of me half the cabin exploded in a shower of glass and smashed mahogany.

Mercifully Lynne had been in a crouching position and, together with Inahara and I, appeared to have escaped injury.

Expecting him to be dead, I looked for John.

His face smothered in blood he turned round to check on the rest of us.

Dropping my rifle I rose to help him but he grinned, gave me a thumbs up sign and returned to his steering.

If we didn't make the protection of the islands in a matter of seconds it was going to be all over. Another salvo like that with the Oerlikon's sights a fraction lower and we'd wind up as bloody pulp in the bottom of a sinking launch.

Filled with foreboding and so scared I couldn't hold my rifle properly, I reloaded and kept trying.

Ten seconds later the first green island rocketed past the port bow. Then another and another. I'd never been more glad to see land in my life.

Abandoning the rifle I crawled forwards into what remained of the wheel-house to see how badly John had been hurt.

Rather to my surprise he still wore the Hyland grin on his face.

"Just a cut," he yelled above the roar of the engines. "That's what they always say, isn't it? Is everyone else okay?"

I nodded. "Christ knows how but I think so."

"Nearly home," he shouted. "Hang on, old buddy."

Heading for a large almost circular island he threaded the Nova through a gap marginally wider than our hull then began edging closer and closer to the overhanging rock wall until the launch was skimming past it only inches away.

Well inside the protection of the islands now there was

no way of knowing what had happened to the Ouvea. If she'd chosen the same island and her crew were trying the same trick in the opposite direction there was going to be one hell of a crash any second from now.

Without slackening speed John did half a lap before veering off at a tangent towards another chunk of rock, hugging the wall again until he was ready for the next jump.

Leapfrogging from one island to another we shot around corners at suicidal speed expecting to confront the Ouvea at every turn. Twice John touched submerged rocks and twice we escaped with no more than a severe scraping.

Then, ten minutes away from Koror where there would be too many people for the Ouvea to finish off what she'd begun, she suddenly appeared in front of us.

But this time we were chasing her and the Oerlikon couldn't fire rearwards through her own superstructure.

Immediately, Inahara was busy with his rifle, his head and shoulders sticking through the ruins of our cabin whilst he fired as rapidly as he could pull the trigger.

For perhaps fifteen seconds, at reasonably close range, we both pumped bullets into the Ouvea's cabin but it was impossible to judge whether we'd been able to inflict any damage and, shortly after we'd begun the attack, I saw Lynne spread her hands to show we'd exhausted our ammunition supply.

But it looked as though we'd done enough.

Travelling at colossal speed, the Ouvea sped away into one of the wider channels, showing every intention of heading out into less congested waters. We were too close to home and I guessed some of our shots must have at last shown them that, despite their bloody Oerlikon, they were not invincible.

They had so nearly destroyed us, killed us for whatever lay inside the sunken Piper, but their attempt had failed and miraculously—incredibly—we were alive, free from serious injury and the Nova was still afloat with engines running.

Face masked in blood, John throttled back the diesels.

Lynne collapsed weakly onto our only intact seat and Inahara stared at me without his usual smile of triumph. He threw his rifle over the side. The gesture was not worthy of him but, in the circumstances, human enough. I thought we had been unbelievably lucky.

"I must apologise," Inahara said quietly. "I had no information which could have prevented this from occurring. It is entirely my fault. Now, Mr Hyland, please be kind enough to take us into Koror where I will leave you in order to seek reinforcements. The situation is far worse than I had anticipated. We must return to the aircraft as rapidly as possible and conclude our business. To do so it appears necessary to find a way of destroying their admirable weapon."

"You really alright, John?" I asked.

"Scalp wound, I think, Doesn't hurt and I can't feel anything—not brains enough to do any damage."

Lynne got up and went to him. "Let me see, John."

I found a cigarette and puffed on it wondering who or what had been looking after us during our extraordinary flight back to the shelter of Palau's Rock Islands.

I've never thought of myself as being brave. I wasn't trying to prove anything to myself or to anyone else and I'd had enough of this whole damn thing. But for the fact I was curious about what I'd pull out of the Piper I think I would have abandoned the mission here and now. I was also conscious of a peculiar stubbornness inside me urging me to see it through and a stupid irrational feeling that I shouldn't let Inahara down—even though I knew he'd lied to me.

Lynne had swabbed most of the blood from John's face and she was rinsing a towel over the stern. When she'd finished she came to stand beside me and took hold of my hand. It was time I admitted it to myself—Lynne Webster had grown so important to me that I was almost scared to consider my feelings. All of the doubt had gone and I was left with a wanting I hadn't experienced since Jean had been alive.

Like a pair of school kids, neither of us inclined to speak, we continued holding hands until we arrived back at the jetty.

John switched off the engines and leaned back against a bulkhead. "Now what?" he said wearily.

Inahara used his shirt to dry his sub-machine gun. "Please take this, Mr Chase. I am going to summon assistance. It will take some hours and it may not be until tomorrow before I can return. I can rely on you, I know."

He stepped onto the ladder on the jetty then turned back to say something else. "I thank you all." He really sounded as though he meant it. There was a smile then he continued his climb to disappear from view.

"Sandwiches," Lynne announced. "If they're still in one piece, that is." She seemed completely recovered from our recent experience.

"You've either got used to all this or you're suffering shock," I said.

She shrugged. "Perhaps it's just that it doesn't matter anymore. Perhaps it's something else."

Avoiding John's eyes I busied myself helping him clear up some of the mess whilst Lynne rummaged around in the ruined cabin. She'd taken some of the bandages from her arm and seemed to be managing well enough.

"How do you fancy another boat trip?" John asked me quietly.

"If you mean sneaking back out to the transmitter to make a dive before Inahara gets back—no thanks. Our radio's bust anyway."

He grinned. "Even if the radio was okay I don't think trying to find the Piper would be too smart, either. Those bastards will be waiting for sure. I had a longer trip in mind." He handed me a piece of thick paper. It was soaked in water and very dirty.

It was a copy of the Palau District map we'd been using but this one had more than the position of the aircraft marked on it. On the western boundary of the reef, over twenty miles south of Koror, someone had drawn another cross. Beside it in Inahara's neat printing, was written: SUB. 374802. 57ft.

I glanced up at John. "Where the hell did you get this?"

"On the floor of the cabin. How about taking a look at the sub?"

I couldn't really see what use there'd be in exploring a World War II submarine which had already given up its secret, but there was something in my head trying to persuade me to agree to his suggestion.

"You never know what goodies those other guys might've missed," he said seriously.

"Suppose we run into trouble again?"

"How can we? The sub's nowhere near the Piper and who's going to see us leave? Come on, old buddy, it's about time we did some finding out for ourselves."

"We'll find out when I get inside the plane."

"I thought you wanted some answers before that?"

I lit another cigarette, inspected the scrap of paper again and tried to make up my mind.

A minute later I'd decided. "Inahara said he might be away until tomorrow. If he isn't back before dark we'll go. We can be out there in a couple of hours and if we wait until then we know damn well no-one will see us."

"And how the hell are we going to find it in the dark?"

"I'll follow the reef on a planing board and use lights if they're still okay. We'll be able to get pretty close by using the compasses so long as we can still see the mainland — okay, okay, I'll compromise. We'll aim to get there at dusk. What about the compasses?"

He held them out. "Unbroken. You're a cautious bastard, Daniel."

I smiled at him. "And everyday I spend on this job makes me sure I'm right. How about you telling Lynne what we're up to while I see if I've got any diving gear left below."

Inevitably, ten minutes later, I had second thoughts about the trip but managed to convince myself that nothing could go wrong so long as we were careful. And I was as anxious to see the sub as John was.

A planing board is a very simple piece of equipment but, underwater in complete darkness with only a very directional beam of light to guide me, it had serious limitations.

Lying flat on the glass fibre board with the lamp in front of me, I was being towed along the edge of a coral cliff at about two knots. We'd jury rigged the device on our way out here to the reef and the extra weight of the lamp housing and the batteries was making the board difficult to control. Planing boards are not designed to be used at night and are certainly not intended to house batteries.

At a depth of eighty feet, close to the bottom, I skimmed over a patch of pure white sand like a piece of live bait at the end of a giant fishing line. Even in daylight, being towed always generates a slight feeling of disquiet and I'd seen divers on boards spending half their time looking over their shoulder to check they weren't being followed by something unpleasant.

At night, with a forward facing light, there was no point in worrying about what might be behind me and I was too old and cynical to be concerned about sharks.

I was only using standard scuba gear although I'd taken the precaution of wearing a wet suit which I hoped might offer some protection if I was unlucky enought to graze the coral. Although two knots didn't sound very fast, and John had expressed surprise at the low speed I'd asked for, with only a narrow reference provided by my light it felt as though I was flying along the reef at a hundred miles an hour.

It had been a while since I'd done any diving at all and several years since I'd been down at night. The total lack of colour in an environment which by day would be a riot of pinks, reds and greens, gave Palau's western reef a slightly sinister quality and I wasn't enjoying the trip much. Even the fish I disturbed seemed to have a rather evil look about them and at the far extremity of my light beam some of the coral formation appeared positively frightening.

This was the second pass along this part of the reef I'd made, the first having proved fruitless, although a couple of times I'd been almost certain I'd found what I was looking for. I knew it would be very difficult to recognise the outline of a submarine which had rested here for so many lonely years. It would be encrusted with marine growth and I could remember plenty of daytime dives when I'd just about swum into sunken boats before I'd known they were there.

We'd bargained on locating the sub right on the very edge of the reef where the chart had shown it, but now I was beginning to have my doubts. Despite the fact that the sun had sunk below the horizon half an hour before we'd arrived, our compass fix had been excellent and rather naively, I suppose, I'd somehow expected to find the vessel right away. My confidence had evaporated quickly enough once I'd seen the real extent of the reef and by now I'd resolved to abandon the job if I couldn't locate it on this second sweep. We didn't know how accurate Inahara's chart might be, the submarine had been blending into the scenery for at least thirty years and it was bloody dark.

Lifting the nose of the board I let myself be towed upwards, dwarfed by the sheer wall of coral to my left until my depth guage read sixty feet exactly. Then I flattened out and peered through my mask into the distance.

Rocks loomed up out of nowhere and I collided with a huge sea anemone trying to avoid smashing into them. There were several frantic seconds of clawing whilst I tried to straighten the board and stop the slewing motion I'd started. More rocks appeared, then a pair of strange looking things resembling four foot high cauliflowers flashed by my left shoulder.

My aqualung cylinders had shifted on my back. As I wriggled to reseat the webbing I happened to glance downwards.

Desperately I fumbled with the cord release to free the board from the tow line and unclipped the illuminated marker from my belt. More by luck than anything I'd found what we were looking for.

From the sudden reduction in drag, John would know I'd let go the line and he'd immediately begin searching for my tiny beacon which was already on its way to the surface. I could imagine his frustration at having to wait on board the Nova now he knew I was on to something.

I'd overshot the place where I'd glimpsed the ugly shape of the submarine and I figured I'd have to go back about fifty or sixty feet to find it again.

The batteries for my light were too heavy for the planing board and without the tow line to pull it along it had become extremely unwieldy. Still lying on it, far more excited than I'd expected I'd be, I kicked myself round and headed downwards.

Slowly scanning the light beam from side to side, I searched for what I was sure had been a conning tower.

And there it was. A huge steel cylinder outlined clearly against the reef.

Something was very wrong, but it took several seconds for the message to finally sink in.

What lay before me was certainly not a World War II Japanese submarine.

Black and gleaming, stretching away further than my

light would reach, the hull was vast with only a trace of marine life adhering to its steel skin. It was huge, evil and bore no resemblance whatever to a 1940 Japanese submarine.

My heart racing, I swam further away from the reef then pointed my light back to gain an overall impression of the shape.

There was not the slightest doubt.

But for a jagged hole cut through the side of the conning tower, it appeared undamaged and I knew I could have stumbled on something not just of importance to John, Lynne and me, but something of vital significance on perhaps an international scale.

Scanning my light rearwards over the hull, I picked out some lettering just aft of the main superstructure. It confirmed my worst suspicions. In clear white letters, four feet high, I read US NAVY 374802.

I checked my watch. Ten minutes of air left but the damn batteries were failing fast. Two new cylinders, a set of replacement batteries and I'd be back to explore properly with John to help me.

Almost unable to believe what I'd found, I took one last look then struck out for the surface to relay the news of my astounding discovery to the others on board the Nova.

I beat my own stream of bubbles to the top, spat out my mouthpiece and started shouting at the dark shape of the Nova floating two hundred yards away.

Her engines started at once, the noise of them sounding peculiarly loud after the silence I'd become accustomed to after being underwater for so long.

It was tempting to yell out before she reached me but I contained my excitement and waited until I could grab the ladder and haul myself on board.

To make it easier for him to locate me once I came up, John had extinguished all his lights. For the moment I could see neither him nor Lynne in the cabin.

"Jackpot," I announced jubilantly. "Guess what's down there."

John came out to help me unhitch my cylinders.

Something hit me in the stomach with such force that every scrap of air was driven from my lungs. Gasping and retching, I collapsed on deck with the whole world spinning round in a sickening whirl of red and white flashes.

THIRTEEN

Semi-conscious, fighting for the breath my lungs were screaming for and convinced I wasn't going to make it, I arched my body backwards.

Someone kicked me savagely behind the ear, following up with another to the small of my back.

Still I couldn't get the oxygen I needed.

On the point of blacking out completely, my lungs seemed to suddenly recover from their paralysis. Twisting about in the cockpit like a freshly caught fish, I sucked greedily at the air until the flashing lights became less vivid and the awful aching in my chest had reduced to a more bearable level.

Hands clutched at my wet suit, lifting me to my feet and pushed me stumbling through the hatchway.

The lights were on now illuminating a nightmarish scene inside the cabin.

Bleeding profusely from his mouth, his face terribly cut and bruised, John tried to raise a Hyland grin. He spat out a piece of tooth and shook his head at me.

There were four men in the cabin with him. Bishop, French and two others.

I stared at them uncomprehending. Then, through the smashed cabin top, I saw the riding lights of the Ouvea where she lay at anchor nearby.

God, they'd followed us. Waited until I'd gone on my dive and then taken over the Nova.

Frantically I looked for Lynne.

Eyes wide with terror, she was crying in a corner with

her blouse torn wide open exposing her breasts. The bandages on her arm were soaked in blood where her wounds had opened up.

"You filthy bastards," I yelled, "what have you done!"

Ignoring the pain from my stomach, I lurched forwards but another shove from behind made me trip. Before I could regain balance both my wrists were seized by the men Inahara had nearly throttled to death.

French's neck was blue and swollen making him appear uglier than I remembered, but Inahara's powerful fingers had done an even better job on Bishop. It looked as though he'd been savaged by an animal, she skin showing the pattern of Inahara's grip in dreadful purple lines running from one ear to the other.

As Bishop started twisting my left arm the man who had shoved me entered the cabin.

"Don't do that," he instructed curtly. "We need him."

He was a neatly dressed European of about thirty with a fine boned face and a small beard. There was a strange air of authority about him. He blinked at me in the light, turning his attention briefly to John and Lynne before speaking to me.

"So we meet at last, Mr Chase," he said. "Did you enjoy your dive?"

Struggling to contain my fury at what they'd done to my friends, I wrenched myself away from the men who held me and advanced towards him.

No apprehension or fear showed in his face and I realised I was confronting a man very different to either Bishop or French.

"What the bloody hell do you think you're doing?" I said, trying to moderate my voice. "And what are you doing on board?"

He smiled at me. A cold humourless smile from a man who knew he'd won. "An accident. I had intended to try to locate the aircraft without your help. I was fairly sure you'd marked its location and hoped to discover your buoy. Unfortunately one of your rifle bullets had holed our fuel tank forcing us to return to Koror for repairs. We were on our way back there when we saw the Nova leaving again. So, with a wooden plug to stop the leak in our tank and having taken on more fuel, we followed you out here, Chase. I'm afraid it was all rather easy."

He spoke public school English and I didn't need anyone to tell me that I was dealing with a man who was perhaps a match for Inahara in the deadly game we'd all been playing.

With Inahara on shore and with John horribly beaten up, the end of everything seemed pretty close. Grossly outnumbered, I couldn't hope to make a fight of it. After so many narrow escapes it was hard to accept an end like this.

"Do you have to behave like bloody animals?" I said to him. "So you've won—okay—but what the hell do you stand to gain by killing us?"

He was in complete control. His own men were waiting for instructions, leaving us to consider what lay in store over the next few hours or minutes.

From the corner of my eyes I saw Lynne gather the ragged edges of her blouse together. By the minute, fear was replacing my anger as I realised we were entirely at the mercy of the calm, cold man standing before me.

He nodded at Bishop and French. "You already know these two. My other colleagues here on the Nova are Mr Nesler and Mr Shulman, both from the United States. My name is Addison; I imagine it means nothing to you. I have spent a lot of time and money on this project, Chase. We can behave as we wish. You must appreciate that Inahara has angered some of my men and they are eager for revenge. Why should I stop them?"

"Leave the girl alone," I snarled. "You've killed her husband—for Christ's sake isn't that enough for you?"

Addison ignored the remark. "Did you locate the submarine?"

"Yes, I did. Inahara told me it was a World War II model with a cargo of Japanese diamonds. I already knew it wasn't carrying diamonds and now I know it isn't a Jap sub." I glanced at John. "US Navy, about five years old and its only been stuck on the reef down there for months, not thirty years."

Addison was visibly amused. "Diamonds. Inahara is more inventive than I gave him credit for. I can see I must explain how seriously you've been misled. I'm not sure Inahara or I would have bothered if the cargo had been diamonds."

"What was it then?" I asked.

"Why heroin, of course. A rather large shipment destined for the United States. I might say a small fortune."

Even at this late stage of events the news rocked me back on my heels. "Heroin!"

"Yes, Chase, heroin. Don't look so surprised. I am in the heroin business and the consignment in the Piper Aztec is mine."

"And Inahara?" I asked quietly.

"Inahara's been trying to lay his hands on it ever since he heard of my arrangements."

"All this has been for heroin?" I said weakly.

"We've spent thousands of dollars on this, Chase. Nothing but heroin or cocaine could justify the kind of expenditure in this day and age. Now, enough of your questions. You will now take us to the aircraft and make the dive you came here to do."

With so many questions racing through my brain I couldn't come to terms with the horrendous fact that we'd all become involved in this for the sick drug trade which was spreading through the world like a rotten disease. Dear God, what a fool I'd been.

"We didn't find the plane," I said.

"That's what Hyland said. And Mrs Webster, too. We were making certain they were telling the truth when you returned from your exploration of the reef. I'm afraid we don't believe you."

John wiped his mouth on his sleeve. "I've already told them, Daniel, but I figure that even if we did know they could still go screw themselves. What do you say, old buddy?"

French's fist thudded into his face. And then again.

This time I steeled myself. "Leave him, French," I shouted. "Addison tell him to stop that—tell him, man!"

John crumpled into a heap. They let Lynne crawl over to him.

"Where is it, Chase?" Addison spoke softly.

"You lousy shit," I breathed. "Out there somewhere. I've told you we don't know for sure."

His face hardened. "We'll see. Go and get in the dinghy. We're going back to the Ouvea."

I did as he asked. For as long as he thought he could make use of my diving ability we'd stay alive. If necessary, to buy some extra time, I'd tell him about the transmitter —anything to buy time whilst I tried to force my numbed brain to function properly.

I was escorted into the tender from the Ouvea, Lynne following me down the ladder nursing her bloodstained arm.

Once we were seated I put my arm round her. "Hold on, Lynne," I said softly, "it's not over yet."

She buried her head on my lap.

Joining us in the dinghy, Nesler and Schulman both trained guns on us whilst three of the crates containing my diving equipment were lowered from the Nova. Then French started the outboard and ran us over to the Ouvea where the crates were transferred. Two Palau islanders helped us on board leaving the tender to return to the Nova for the others.

Still holding Lynne, I attempted to overcome the feeling of despair which was threatening to engulf me. Inahara had betrayed us, employed us, lied to us yet we'd believed in him. It was utterly inconceivable, but now, thinking back over the last few days and nights, what had there been to substantiate his claim of representing the Japanese Government. Nothing—bloody nothing. And we'd never asked him. He'd fooled us as if we were children—children in the hands of an experienced international drug trader. The knowledge was awful.

When the dinghy returned from its second trip, John was not among the passengers.

"Hyland," I said to Addison. "Where's John Hyland?"

"He's going to stay on the Nova. We don't need him anymore."

For a second I was afraid they might have killed him, but then I saw his sillhouette moving against the dim lights in the Nova's cabin. He'd recovered from the blows he'd received from French.

Lifting the anchor, men were beginning to ready the Ouvea for sea and I heard the rumble as our engines started.

Apart from her red and green riding lights, the Ouvea was still in complete darkness preventing me from seeing what was happening on board with any certainty. But I could see the Nova clearly enough now. I imagined they'd sabotaged her engines but John would stand a good chance of being picked up sometime tomorrow providing he could hold himself together for what remained of the night. Without knowing how badly he'd been hurt, I wasn't sure if he was in need of medical attention or not, but he was pretty tough and, on balance he was probably luckier than Lynne and I were. I was very concerned that Addison had decided that Lynne should accompany us, although the reason was painfully obvious.

Addison was speaking to me.

"What?" I said.

"The aircraft, Chase. The Piper, where is it?"

"For Christ's sake, I've told you twice already. I don't know."

"The last time, Chase. Where?"

I didn't answer. Then suddenly I realised. But I was much too late. A lifetime too late.

Addison shouted a single command and the Oerlikon hammered into life. On board in the dark, the muzzle flash was tremendous.

Backwards and forwards across the Nova, high velocity 20mm shells pounded her at almost point blank range, smashing her hull, her engines and her broken cabin until she was no more than a floating pile of wreckage.

Only at the very end did flames begin billowing outwards from her ruptured fuel tanks to slowly envelop what was left of her. A funeral pyre for the young man who had been my friend.

Fighting wildly to get to Addison, I was going to kill him for what he'd done. It took the combined strength of four of them to hold me back.

Addison stared unmoving at the dying flames for a moment then turned to face me.

"We still have Mrs Webster," he said coldly. "Now will you take us to the aircraft?"

"You heathen bloody killer," I shouted. "You murdering son of a bitch. As God is my witness I shall kill you for this, Addison."

"Answer my question."

I looked at Lynne and looked into the icy eyes of the man who held all the aces. There was only one answer I could give him.

FOURTEEN

Shaking with fury at Addison's unnecessary brutality, I clenched both hands round one of the Ouvea's hand rails in order to prevent myself from trying to attack him again. But for the knowledge that Lynne's life depended solely on me remaining calm, I don't believe I would've been able to contain the terrible need to avenge John's death.

As it was, once I'd made my dive, what was there to stop Addison putting a bullet through our heads? I'd seen enough to know he was devoid of all compassion and there was no reason for him to keep us alive once he'd got his hands on the heroin. Twenty miles from here, Addison was going to force me to bring up the drug consignment from the plane and then it would be all over.

I thought of Gerry, of Lynne's husband and of John Hyland — all murdered, sacrificed for a cache of heroin which would cause more misery in the world than most people could even begin to comprehend. I had to prevent this man from causing such suffering, but I was helpless.

To stop it from happening I could refuse to dive. If I did, I could imagine the persuasive measures they'd use on Lynne and, anyway, I knew resistance was futile. Sooner or later they'd find the sunken plane whether I helped them or not. Unless, of course, Inahara would finally beat them at their own game.

At the very thought of Inahara my fury returned. Sweat broke out on my forehead as I realised how I'd been used.

Lynne moved closer to my side. "Stop blaming yourself,"

she whispered. "We're dealing with animals, not people. You couldn't know they were going to kill John."

"I've got to make the dive, Lynne. You know why, don't you?"

"Yes, but I want you to know I'll understand if you decide not to."

"It'll keep us alive for another two hours," I said grimly. "I'll spin it out as long as I can."

"Two hours isn't going to help us, is it?"

I had no answer to give her. Apart from a suicide pact, what else could we do? Fate had dealt us an impossible hand and I knew there was nothing for it but to make up my mind to go through with the dive. Maybe Addison would relent and let us live—a slim possibility, but any possibility was better than the certain death his men would mete out if I tried to kill him before we reached the transmitter.

The flames from the Nova's wreckage were too far away to be seen now and already the Ouvea was winding her way between the sparsely scattered Rock Islands which extended this far south. Using a bow mounted spot lamp to pick out the safest passage through them, we were travelling fast at close to twenty knots. Less than an hour from now we'd be at the place where the Piper was supposed to lie.

Addison had come aft to speak to me. The bastard knew I couldn't touch him and for a second, as he approached, it took all my self control to prevent myself from having one last go at tearing out his throat.

"Okay, Chase, for the last time, where is it?"

"We marked where we think it is with a radio transmitter," I said dully. "But I don't know how close it is to the plane. If Hyland's calculations were wrong we could be miles out. You're stupid if you expect me to find it in the dark."

"You found the submarine easily enough. We'll locate

the transmitter tonight, you can make a couple of dives as soon as we arrive."

"And if it's not there?"

"Carry on in the morning. With Mrs Webster on board I'm sure you're going to try very hard."

I unclenched my hands and started stripping off my wet suit to keep cool. "What's the hurry?"

"You know as well as I do: Don't pretend to be stupid. Inahara will be back and next time, perhaps, our gun won't frighten him off."

Dropping the top half of my suit onto the deck I reluctantly accepted a cigarette from him. Somehow or other I was going to kill him but first I had to find a way and I'd never needed a cigarette more in my life.

"Tell me about that sub, Addison, what happened to it?" I heard the shake in my voice.

He placed a foot on the rail, studying the glowing tip of his own cigarette. "Rather an interesting story. It was an ordinary US submarine, not a nuclear model or anything like that. The only strange thing is that it was damn near brand new. Nine months ago it was delivered to Japan from the States but it suffered two major accidents inside the first month the Japs had it. In the second one, fourteen people were gassed inside and the Americans agreed to take it back to San Diego for a complete check-out.

The US Navy flew out a skeleton crew to make sure nothing went wrong on the trip home but I'm pleased to say they didn't do a very thorough job when they chose their men. Without knowing, the Navy got themselves in the position of delivering the largest single shipment of heroin I've ever had the good luck to handle.

Nesler and Shulman organised the US end of it and I fixed the main contract up from Hong Kong, moving the stuff out of the Philippines by small boats. The sub made pre-arranged collection rendezvous at dozens of different places before taking off for San Diego. Then, right here on

Palau's reef, the bloody thing went wrong again. Nesler got a single coded radio message giving its last position and that was that."

It was very nearly as extraordinary as the story Inahara had told us. But this one was true and, unlike Inahara, he wasn't trying to talk me into anything. He didn't have to.

He continued speaking. "I flew out a whole damn team of people from the UK to get the heroin up before anyone started looking for the sub. Webster of course was our diver before he got cute. I hired Bishop and French in Guam because of their local experience—they've been pushing drugs out here in the islands for years. About the time we heard of Inahara everything began going wrong. Inahara got really interested and started poking about in the Philippines while we were out here on Palau—then, two days after we were ready to pull out, our wretched plane crashed just after it had left the airstrip. Absolutely bloody incredible luck. Anyway, that's where you and Hyland got yourselves tied up with Inahara—you know the rest. For four million bucks worth of heroin you can spend a lot of money, Chase, but this has cost an unbelievable amount. There's one thing I can promise you though—this time we're not going to lose out. Nesler and Shulman are here to make sure of it."

"So you're still intending to ship the stuff to the States?" I asked.

He shook his head. "That was the whole idea behind the submarine. Nobody would've expected the American Navy to smuggle four million dollars worth of heroin into the States. No, Chase, this time it's going south into Australia. We've got people ready in Guam, they'll get it on board Japanese fishing boats, Russian trawlers—any small vessel bound for the north Australia coast. The market down there is growing all the time."

"What about Inahara?" I asked.

"Just another bastard pirate. The hard drug business is

full of them. He got a tip from somewhere and he's looking for a fast buck like everyone else. He's spent a lot of money, too, but let me tell you there's no way he's going to break in on my deal. He's tough but not tough enough for this one."

"What are you going to do about us if I find the plane?" I said quietly.

"Not if, when."

"Answer my question."

"We'll see. I suppose we could chuck you over the side to give you a chance. Maybe you deserve a chance like that — maybe."

I ground my teeth together. "I can choose not to find it."

He shook his head. "Not so long as my men are enjoying themselves with Mrs Webster — you won't like that, Chase — I can tell. You'll find it."

"I can't guarantee that; even Hyland wasn't sure he'd found the right place."

He swivelled round. "I said you'll find it." He reached out and ripped open Lynne's torn blouse. "You won't do anything but dive, Chase," he said softly. "And you'll locate the plane — is that clear?"

Through a film I watched Lynne use her good arm to try and stop him but he laughed at her ineffective struggles and pushed her into my arms.

Sobbing, she clutched at me as if I could save her. But I could not for I was powerless before this empty man who had stated that we had only the slimmest chance of living once I'd done what had been asked of me.

Watching him return to the wheel house, for the first time ever, I knew how it felt to want to rip another human being apart with my bare hands.

Twenty minutes later Addison told me they'd picked up the first signals from the transmitter. I hadn't told him the frequency but the Ouvea carried the same model of radio that had been fitted to the Nova and I'd known it would be a simple matter for them to make a frequency sweep until they received the bleeps from the sea bed.

I watched French lash Lynne's wrists to the hand rail whilst other members made ready to drop the anchor.

"We'll give you power for the light from our main batteries," Addison said. "It'll reach about two hundred feet. If it's deeper than that you'll have to come back for a portable one."

"Don't worry," I said. "I'm only going to use the aqualung to start with. If it's really a long way down I'll be back for some proper gear, anyway. Have you anybody who knows what to do if I want pumped air and a full suit?"

He nodded. "Both the island boys. And we've got deep sea equipment if you want it. We shipped most of our original machinery back to the UK once we'd found the sub, but we had to fly some more out for Webster to use when the plane crashed."

"I know," I said. "I saw it on Guam on the way here."

"Didn't do you any good, did it?" Bishop said. "You're all eyes and mouth, aren't you big boy."

I ignored the remark, peeling on my wet suit again and slipping into the harness on my air cylinders.

"What exactly am I looking for if I find the Piper?" I asked Addison.

"Four plastic containers. They'll be stowed in the tail somewhere."

Four, I thought bitterly. Four containers of heroin, not diamonds. A brand new American submarine, not a rusted out World War II Japanese hulk. It was all so nearly as I'd been told by oh so very different.

Before I put in my mouthpiece I went over to talk to Lynne. Taking her face in my hands, I kissed her firmly on the mouth. Her lips were warm and salty and tears were streaming down her cheeks.

"We'll make it," I promised her. "All the time they think I can help them we're both safe—just remember that. I'll see you in a little while. I'll be thinking of you while I'm down there."

Picking up the heavy lamp I lowered it into the water on the end of its cord, gave Lynne a final glance then prepared for the dive.

The period I'd already spent underwater on the planing board earlier tonight had accustomed me to the dark world beneath the Ouvea. Tilting the light downwards I swam steadily into the black void below me, almost grateful to be alone where I could think.

Although my stomach was still painful where Addison had slugged me, I felt reasonably fit and began to regain some badly needed confidence. I had no intention of even looking for the Piper but in case they could see the light from up top I had to move around otherwise they'd be certain to guess I was playing for time.

At a depth of sixty feet I saw the pale outline of a Rock Island which hadn't quite made it to the surface. Devoid of seaweed it was curiously flat, looking rather like an enormous table top. I swam towards it until my flippers caught the edge then stood up to look around. Unless I was lucky enough to pick up a reflection from some shiny aluminium, even if John's calculations had been perfect, I wouldn't have been able to see the Piper if it was fifty yards away. The water was clear enough but in the pitch blackness surrounding me all I was likely to discover was something as big as a submarine or something with a light or a reflector on it.

No sooner had the thought crossed my mind than far away to my right, I could have sworn I saw another light.

The notion was absurd. Although my vision could be playing tricks, I was certain it had been brighter than a chance reflection.

Almost unwilling to turn my own light beam in the

direction of what I surely must have imagined, I peered across the submerged island.

The shock of what was there made me drop the lamp.

In apparently perfect condition, illuminated in the eerie glow from some other light source, a neat clinker built boat lay on its side as though it had been drawn up and left there deliberately.

Surprise gave way to irrational terror, Seizing my own light I swiftly pointed it just above the boat to confirm my suspicions.

Contrasting with the white rock plateau, four black shadows were coming towards me.

Grabbing a lead weight from my diving belt in one hand and clasping my light in the other I sprang off the edge of the rock with my heart banging so hard it was difficult to breathe.

Experience came to my aid. Concentrating my beam on one of the shapes, with a tremendous jolt I saw I was not alone. Four men, similarly equipped, were down here with me.

Had Addison sent his crew down to check on me? There hadn't been time. So who were they? And for God's sake where had they come from?

All four had stopped swimming. The one carrying the light was beckoning to me.

Still gripping my weight I allowed myself to sink until I was only a few feet away from him.

Then, through the mask, I saw the eyes of Inahara.

My relief was beyond description. Drug pusher, liar, murderer even but I'd never been so pleased nor so astonished to see anyone.

I thumped him on the back wondering how the hell he'd managed to arrive at such a critical time and how he'd known what had happened.

Taking my arm, he guided me back to the sunken boat where he produced a grease pencil from one of the flooded lockers. Using his own light he wrote a single word on the engine cover.

OUVEA?

I nodded to him. He wrote again.

HOW MANY MEN?

Holding up seven fingers I took the pencil from him to write my own message.

LYNNE ON BOARD. JOHN DEAD.

He showed he understood. From the boat he passed me a wide bladed knife then shone his light on the other three wet suited men who were with him. There was something else he wanted to write.

GET LYNNE DOWN HERE. SHARE AIR. LEAVE REST TO ME.

Indicating that I should leave at once, he made a strange circular motion with his hands to the others then started lifting a small box from the boat. I didn't wait to see what was in it.

Heart still thumping, hardly able to believe that help could have arrived from such an unexpected quarter, I slipped the knife inside my waist band and took off.

French pulled me roughly up the ladder as soon as I reached the Ouvea. As I expected, Addison immediately jumped to the wrong conclusion.

"You've found it!"

I spat out my mouthpiece and looked around for Lynne. Addison shook me by the shoulder. "Is it there, Chase? Is it there?"

"Yes," I said angrily. "Stop shoving me around and for Christ's sake untie her. She's not going anywhere."

He shouted a command to Nesler who reluctantly freed Lynne's hands from the rail. She ran over to me.

I had to make them believe everything was going to plan.

"You'll have to give me a hatchet or something," I said to Addison. "The tail's all smashed up and I can't get into the fuselage."

"Mind you don't hole one of the containers, they might be close to the skin." Addison was visibly excited.

"I'll mind. Where's the hatchet?"

As he half turned to shout another instruction I grasped Lynne's hand so I knew where she was. It was time.

Addison's words turned to a scream as my knife sank to its hilt in his soft belly.

For Gerry, for John and, because of all the men I'd ever known, he deserved to die. I yanked upwards with the blade and left him to his agony.

Lifting Lynne by the waist I threw her bodily over the side and jumped after her. There was a last glimpse of the Ouvea before I forced my mouthpiece between her teeth, shouted my brief instructions in her ear and dragged her under.

Two long breaths for her—wait until she's ready—take the mouthpiece from her and breathe myself. Give it back to her, can't find her mouth—God it's dark. Two more breaths—my turn again. Keep kicking, pull her down deeper—get her hair out of her mouth. Down and down, no light, no sound but the bubbles and only one mouthpiece for both of us.

The technique wasn't working. She must be gulping water each time I transferred the mouthpiece. I felt her growing limp in my arms.

It was no good. I'd have to get her up before she drowned. It was the bloody lagoon all over again.

Still sharing the mouthpiece with Lynne getting weaker by the second, I kicked furiously with my flippers driving us upwards to the air.

Fifteen feet from the surface the whole sky flashed a brilliant orange. Simultaneously a shock wave took hold of us as though we were pieces of cork.

My eardrums seemed to explode inside my head and Lynne was wrenched from my grasp.

FIFTEEN

I should never have doubted him. From the very first meeting I'd been impressed with his complete professionalism and, against a man like Inahara, Addison had been no more than an amateur who had paid the ultimate price for a performance which hadn't been good enough.

With Lynne cradled in my arms, I lay back against the wet rubber of the dinghy, closed my eyes and wondered that we were still alive.

We'd been much too close to the surface when the Ouvea had blown up and as I'd lost consciousness I could remember thinking what a bloody shame it was that we were both going to drown after so nearly making it.

In fact, although the shock wave from the explosion had hammered Lynne pretty badly, I'd since discovered that she hadn't blacked out at all. They'd dragged her out of the water first and hadn't bothered about retrieving me too quickly because of my diving experience. When they eventually hauled me into the life raft I was badly waterlogged and it'd taken the concentrated efforts of Inahara and two others to pump me dry.

That had been several minutes ago. Now, all six of us were packed into the tiny inflatable dinghy waiting for the blazing stern section of the Ouvea to disappear from sight. Lit by the flames, wreckage from the blast floated all around us and, from the size of the bits and pieces, I knew there was little point in searching for survivors.

Addison was dead—the only man I'd ever killed in cold blood—yet I felt no remorse, no shame for what I'd done.

Opposite me, Inahara was struggling out of his harness, a huge chunk of a man who had driven the Ouvea's entire crew to eternity. I could partially see his face in the light from the flames. For different reasons, he too was unmoved and detached from the deaths he had caused.

Drug trader he might be, but without him Lynne and I would almost certainly have died at the hands of Addison. Inahara had saved us—maybe because he still wanted me to dive for the heroin—but in time perhaps I could come to terms with that. Right now it didn't matter.

Five hundred yards away the flames were abruptly extinguished and there was a gentle sucking sound as the remains of the Ouvea vanished forever.

"And so it is done, Mr Chase," Inahara said, breaking the silence. "Are you and Mrs Webster quite comfortable?"

"I'm a bit cold," Lynne said, "but we're both alright."

She was the only one of us without a wet suit and even though the night was warm enough the shock could be having an effect on her.

Inahara took off the jacket of his suit to wrap it round her shoulders.

"How the hell did you know, Inahara?" I asked him. "How did you manage it?"

"Ah, Daniel, you were surprised to see me, were you not?"

The use of my christian name again—why? "I wasn't just surprised," I said. "Scared to hell to start with—then I didn't believe it. You've got no idea how glad I was to recognise you, Inahara. Things were pretty grim. They were going to kill us after I'd got the heroin for them. They'd already killed John in the Nova and we were next."

"So Addison told you about the heroin?"

"He did. Which makes you a lying bastard, doesn't it."

"Indeed, but it is all over now, Daniel."

I wasn't exactly sure what he meant by that but I certainly wasn't going to start making trouble. There'd be time to decide what to do once we got back to Koror. "Come on, Inahara," I said, "I'm too damn tired to guess — what about the boat down there?"

There was a gleam of teeth in the dark. "Perhaps more than you think, Daniel. You and Mrs Webster have been lucky — very lucky. I will explain to you whilst we wait."

"Wait for what?"

"Be patient, my friend. One matter at a time. When I returned to the wharf at Koror with my colleagues late yesterday evening, I of course found the Nova missing. Although unable to bring myself to believe the three of you had decided to doublecross me, I knew there was only one place you could have gone. Why you had chosen to be so stupid as to return to the transmitter when you knew Addison would be waiting, I could not imagine. However, I had no option but to follow you by boat and pray that neither of us would encounter the Ouvea at sea.

On arrival here I was astonished to find no sign of the Nova, but of course, in the dark, it was difficult to determine whether you were nearby or not. It would have been easy for you to have heard us coming on such a still night and I believed you could perhaps be waiting a mile or two away. I chose to ignore the possibility and commenced work.

We had not long found the Piper when one of my colleagues heard a launch approaching so — — —"

"You found it!" Lynne exclaimed.

"Of course, Mrs Webster. Mr Hyland's calculations were extremely accurate. It is a great pity he did not live to learn what a splendid job he had done."

"Don't worry about that," I said. "If John Hyland had known he'd been helping find drugs he'd never have forgiven himself."

"Probably," Inahara replied calmly. "But allow me to continue. As I was saying, in view of the potential danger, I decided to scuttle our own boat and wait to see whether it was the Nova or the Ouvea which had disturbed us. There was little time to make my decision and I was not prepared to risk a further encounter with Addison's gun.

Some minutes later, when I saw the underwater lamp you were using, I knew immediately you were diving from the Ouvea. The remainder of the story is already known to you."

"What happened to the Ouvea?" I asked quietly.

"My friends are also very experienced underwater but in their own way. They brought the equivalent of a limpet mine with them in case we had the good fortune to come across Addison secretly among the islands."

"I killed Addison," I said.

"I know, Daniel. I saw you. I was watching from the water some yards away — it was important to be sure you and Mrs Webster had escaped before setting the fuse. You are a more violent man than I had believed you to be."

"So you blew up the Ouvea with the mine?" Lynne queried.

"Quite so, Mrs Webster. Mr Chase had settled his own score with the man Addison but Nesler and Shulman had to be dealt with and it was necessary for Bishop and French to die. I knew those two for many years — or knew of them. They caused more unhappiness and suffering in the Pacific islands in the last two years than their population has suffered in the past two centuries. Drug addiction is a terrible thing, Mrs Webster. Once you have seen it face to face you can never be the same."

"Christ," I said angrily, "you're a hypocritical bastard. What the hell's the difference between you and them? You might've saved our lives, Inahara, but that doesn't change how I think about you and all of your bloody kind."

None of the other men had said anything since we'd started talking but my outburst had moved one of them. He had a well educated American voice and sounded amused at my anger.

"For someone who's just been saved from what sounds like a real nasty situation, you're not too grateful, Chase."

Lynne placed a hand on my arm. "Daniel, it's not our business and there's nothing more we can do."

"They didn't even need a proper diver," I said bitterly. "The bloody plane couldn't have been in deep water at all. I got fouled up in this for nothing—for bloody nothing."

The man who had addressed me lifted what appeared to be a portable short wave radio from the floor of the dinghy. Pulling out the aerial he operated one of the switches then held the instrument at arms' length above his head.

"And what about this dinghy and the radio?" I asked.

"Carried with us in our boat, of course," Inahara replied. "Once we had disposed of the Ouvea, I automatically inflated the life raft underwater. Mrs Webster will tell you how frightened she was when it came up alongside her in the dark. Naturally we have already used the radio to summon assistance. Captain Beckert is merely sending out a continuous signal to guide the helicopter here."

Captain Beckert? Captain? Helicopter? What the hell was he talking about?

Lynne and I both spoke at once. The man Inahara had called Beckert held up his hand. "Quiet, please." He steadied the radio against his ear for a moment. "All okay, Commander," he said with satisfaction. "They've got us."

The remark had been directed at Inahara. And I'd heard correctly.

"We will all be able to leave together, Captain?" Inahara asked.

"Yeah. Be a tight fit but we'll make it."

From the north the faint noise of a helicopter was throbbing across the Rock Islands.

I tried to stand up but Lynne was lying on me and the

life raft wasn't big enough. "Inahara," I shouted. "Whose helicopter is it?"

Beckert answered. "I guess you could say it belongs to the US Navy, Chase."

"It is a reconnaisance helicopter from the US frigate Colorado, Daniel," Inahara said. "I radioed the Colorado yesterday afternoon and requested urgent official assistance. Captain Beckert and his crew flew it nearly three hundred miles to Palau to conclude this mission. It will take us back to Koror where we will be able to discuss matters in more detail."

I was too stunned to ask for an explanation. It was left to Lynne to express the utter astonishment we both felt. "You work for the Navy?" she said incredulously. "The American Navy?"

Beckert laughed. "Right now the Navy's working for the Commander, Mrs Webster, but you're nearly right. From what the Commander's told us I imagine you're kinda surprised."

Moving very fast, at low altitude the helicopter was close now, the chopping noise growing steadily louder as the pilot homed in on Beckert's radio signal. A mile away its landing lights came on.

"Inahara," I said weakly. "Before it gets here — you've got to tell me — what about the heroin?"

Creating an enormous downdraught the chopper stopped overhead. Inahara had to lean across to shout his answer over the noise from the gas turbine. "As they say in the States, Daniel I am on the side of the angels. Be sure you are among men you would be proud to call your friends. The heroin has been given to the sea. By now every trace of it will have vanished. Now please prepare Lynne for the lifting straps. It will be necessary for us to be winched on board and she should go first. We will speak later."

It took ten hectic and anxious minutes to transfer us from the dinghy to the hovering chopper, ten minutes of being exposed to the fearful blast of air from its rotor whilst the nylon strap went up and down six times. But, once inside the cabin, there was hot soup, unlimited cups of coffee and a badly needed cigarette for those of us who smoked.

Lynne was soon swathed in blankets whilst her arm was inspected and carefully rebandaged by one of the crew. She hadn't stopped smiling yet.

So it had ended, an ending as unexpected and as extraordinary as the startling train of events which had occurred since that fateful night when I'd stepped off the plane in Hawaii. I lay back against a bulkhead and tried to relax.

Grinning, Inahara joined me on the floor. "Right, my friend. Permit me to introduce myself. I am Commander Inahara of US Naval Intelligence. Although of Japanese parentage I am an American and for many years served my Government in the Pacific. On this assignment, until now, I have been forced to work secretly but the reasons for this are perhaps obvious to you?"

"They're not," I said. "But I'm obviously pretty damn stupid. I'm afraid you'd better start at the beginning."

"It is only the beginning you do not already know and I imagine Addison has told you something about the submarine. My mission was simple enough, Daniel — investigate a tip-off that the American Navy was to be used to smuggle a substantial consignment of drugs into the States and determine what had become of submarine 374802. I had instructions to work entirely alone and on no account to involve US officials at any level whatever. Washington was severely upset to learn that the Navy could have been infiltrated in such a way and in order to find the men responsible it was considered essential to keep things absolutely secret. That is why I recruited you and Mr Hyland. You were not only experts in the two fields which concerned my project but as non US citizens with well documented career histories you were beyond suspicion.

"But why on earth didn't you tell us the truth?" I said.

He smiled. "Both of you were what I would call adventurers, Daniel. Men particularly interested in the more unusual and exciting things of life. Had I asked you to officially assist the American Government prevent four million dollars worth of heroin entering the country, you might well have told me to find someone else for the job. The recovery of diamonds was a more attractive proposition, was it not?"

One of the flight crew passed Inahara a sheet of paper and started to say something, but Inahara waved him away and continued with his explanation.

"I had every intention of telling you the truth well before we reached Palau but with Mrs Webster's arrival on the scene and with the difficulties we encountered, the opportunity did not really present itself. I was also concerned that you might have decided to leave the task to the US authorities once you discovered we were not engaged on what could be termed a treasure hunt."

"But why pretend you represented the Japanese Government?" Lynne asked.

"Because I do not look like an American—and because the story about the diamonds was perhaps more believable, certainly more attractive and also easy for me to tell. A true story, Mrs Webster, but one which, with my help, was concluded over two years ago. The other submarine, however, was situated elsewhere in the Pacific."

I was thinking about what he'd said. An adventurer, someone who'd be uninterested in helping the American Government to keep the drugs out of the States, but someone who'd respond to a semi-official request from the Japanese to salvage a hoard of diamonds. I'd never know if Inahara had been right or whether for two thousand dollars a day I'd have agreed to work for the devil himself. It didn't sound like the Daniel Chase I imagined myself to be, but maybe the man I'd become was really the one Inahara had gambled on. It was a vaguely disturbing thought.

With a huge grin on his old graunched face Inahara had finished reading the piece of paper. He stood up and summoned the man who'd given it to him. "This is excellent," Inahara said. "I am most pleased. Please explain how this occurred."

The crewman crouched down to avoid having to shout over the noise from the turbine. "We heard gunfire, sir, and decided we'd better take a look. We couldn't very well miss it — the boat was still burning when we got there. When we got down low enough — there he was — so we just lifted him out of the water and flew him back to Koror. It was as simple as that."

Lynne burst out of her cacoon of blankets. "John," she cried. "Not John?"

I scrambled to my feet hardly daring to wait for Inahara's confirmation.

"Indeed. The note is from him. He is concerned about the money I promised to pay. A very resilient young man Mr Hyland."

He'd made it — John had made it.

Lynne threw herself into my arms. "All of us," she breathed. "And it's all over."

Far below us, the sparse lights of Koror and Babelthuap twinkled like lost diamonds on the black edges of Palau's islands.

Another night landing over the big empty Pacific but one with a difference — an enormous, wonderful difference that I hadn't experienced for a long time. It had finally happened.

Gently pulling her wet hair away from her face, I looked into her extraordinary eyes. And I knew, at last, that things were going to be alright for the rest of my life.